Naughty Holidays

2021

Naughty Holidays 2021

2021

NICOLE EDWARDS

NICOLE EDWARDS LIMITED
A dba of SL Independent Publishing, LLC
PO Box 1086
Pflugerville, Texas 78691

NAUGHTY HOLIDAYS 2021
Nicole Edwards

COVER DETAILS:

Image: © photosvit (66333101) | 123rf
Design: © Nicole Edwards Limited

INTERIOR DETAILS:

Formatting: Nicole Edwards Limited
Editing: Blue Otter Editing | www.BlueOtterEditing.com

IDENTIFIERS:

ISBN: (ebook) 978-1-64418-047-1 | (paperback) 978-1-64418-048-8

BISAC: FICTION / Romance / General

Dedication

This one is dedicated to Nicole Nation.

Dear Reader,

I enjoyed spending time with many of my characters, some I haven't heard from in a really long time. It was so much fun, I decided that it might be time to see what they are up to now.

With that said, you'll find a short story about many of my readers' favorites, and I hope you'll find enjoyment in catching up with them. To take it another step, if you enjoy one of these stories more than the others and would like more about those characters, be sure to visit my website and vote for them. One set of characters from the Naughty Holidays 2021 book will receive a full-length book in 2022. The voting will be open until January 1, 2022.

Much Love,

Nicole Edwards

Table of Contents

Thanksgiving and Wine

Kingston Rush and Ellie Kaufman from *Rush*

Kingston and Ellie are enjoying Thanksgiving with family and friends. Learn why wine is not on the menu and why Ellie needs it more than ever.

Thursday, November 25, 2021

KINGSTON RUSH

"She's bringing a boy to dinner," Ellie says in a bad excuse for a conspiratorial whisper.

I smile at my wife despite the concern I detect in her tone. Ever since my seventeen-year-old stepdaughter, Bianca, asked if she could bring her boyfriend to Thanksgiving dinner, Ellie has been doing her best to hide her nervousness. As for why she's nervous to meet the boy her daughter is dating, I have no idea.

"I heard," I inform her.

"Tonight," she adds.

"Heard that, too."

Ellie peers toward the hallway as though ensuring Bianca isn't standing there listening to our conversation. I could've told her she wasn't because last I saw Bianca, she was pacing her bedroom, fretting over what she was going to wear tonight while tossing one outfit after another onto her bed.

For the record, I will never understand women completely.

"What if he doesn't like us?" Ellie asks, reaching for the bottle of wine she opened a little while ago.

I bark a laugh. "Don't you think it should be the opposite? What if *you* don't like *him?*"

"Me?" Her eyebrows slam down. "I like everyone."

"Maybe. But you've never met one of Bianca's boyfriends."

Her eyes narrow. "She's never had a boyfriend before."

That we know of. Of course, I keep that to myself.

I laugh again and reach for Ellie, pulling her toward me. "It's gonna be fine, baby. One dinner."

She pulls back, stares up at me, her expression one of disbelief. "Only the most important dinner of the entire year."

"And your brother will be here," I tell her. "And Noelle. If anyone can keep Bianca in line, it's Noelle."

Ellie takes a deep breath, blows it out loudly. "True."

I don't bother to mention the additional dozen guests who will be here to keep order in the event Ellie thinks Bianca's boyfriend doesn't like her. He will like her, though. Everyone likes Ellie because she's fucking likable. My entire team adores her, and they're a rowdy bunch of hockey players, so that's saying something.

Wanting to get her mind off of Bianca's boyfriend and everyone else who will be descending on our house this evening, I glance at the oven then return my gaze to her. "Is there anything you need me to do?"

That works because her brain shifts gears, and she is back to fretting over the meal rather than who's attending.

Ellie scans the kitchen, glances at the oven, looks back at me. "No. Not right now. The turkey's got a couple more hours."

A couple of hours?

"And Cason?" I ask, referring to our almost-four-year-old son. "How much longer will he nap?"

"Not quite that long, but close. Why?"

I smile and reach for her, pulling her back to me again. "Then perhaps we should take a shower."

"Together?"

"Yeah," I say, feigning innocence. "You know, to conserve water."

"Right. Water conservation." Her jade-green eyes blaze with familiar heat. "I like the way you think."

"Do you?" I link my fingers with hers and turn toward the bedroom before anyone can interrupt what will be the highlight of my day.

ELLIE RUSH

I love this man.

Even after nearly five years of marriage, I love him so much I can hardly contain it.

And yes, a big part of why I love him is because he does things like this. He offers me a distraction when I need it most. I know it's silly to get all worked up over who is coming to dinner, yet it isn't something that can be helped. And here he is, offering to sex me up just so I don't lose my mind.

Not that I need a reason, because seriously, I am married to Kingston Rush, the rock-star goalie for the Austin Arrows hockey team. He is the sexiest man in hockey—perhaps even in all of professional sports—and I'm not the only one who thinks so. Women love him, but thankfully, he's all mine, no matter how many of them tweet about wanting to climb Mount Rushmore. For the record, I am the only woman in the world who has the honor of doing that.

"What's on your mind?" my husband asks as he all but drags me into the bathroom.

"Climbing Mount Rushmore," I admit honestly.

His smile is slow and wicked and it does crazy things to my insides.

"Have I mentioned that it's suggested that you climb naked?"

I giggle. "Is that so?"

He feigns seriousness when he cants his head and nods. "Yeah. Yeah, I read it somewhere."

I laugh, loving his humor as much as I love his sexiness.

Leaning up on my toes, I meet his lips with my own, sinking into him when he puts his big, warm hands on my back and slowly slides them down to my ass.

"Perhaps you should help me into the right gear then," I suggest.

"Oh, I can definitely do that," he replies against my mouth.

We aren't strangers to undressing one another. In fact, we've gotten pretty good at it over the years. Maybe we're not record-setting good, but it doesn't take long to strip down to nothing, our clothes strewn across the bathroom to be dealt with later.

"I am a huge fan of your climbing gear, Mrs. Rush," he says, his voice a dark rasp against my lips.

"Thank you, Mr. Rush. You think the water's warm yet?"

"We can find out."

Since the bathroom is filling with steam, I have no doubt that it's warm enough, but it doesn't matter, because Kingston's mouth is on mine as he picks me up like I weigh nothing. With practiced ease, I wrap my legs around his waist, my arms around his neck, and hold on as he walks into the enormous shower. I shift and grind against his rigid erection, which is pressed firmly against my clit. While I am a huge fan of foreplay—both as a giver and as a receiver—I know there isn't time for us to dawdle.

Not to mention, I am so worked up, I'm not sure I will survive too much of his wicked ministrations.

"Now, Kingston," I moan against him when he presses my back against the cool tile. "I need you inside me."

He growls softly, shifting so he can slide one hand between our bodies. The next thing I know, his cock is pressed to my entrance, and I am sighing his name as my head tips back against the tile.

Oh, yeah. *This* is what I need. The delicious friction as he slides inside me.

"God, that feels good."

Kingston doesn't rush as he pushes in slow and deep, filling me to overflowing. I squeeze my internal muscles as encouragement, and I get another rumbling growl in response.

"Kiss me, Ellie," he bites out.

Putting my mouth back to his, I meet his tongue with mine. It starts out slow, but it doesn't take much to set me off, and then my husband is ravishing my mouth. His hips begin to thrust faster, forcing me to hold myself still to allow for that perfect penetration.

I succumb to the bliss, focusing solely on the glorious sensation as he fucks me. Slowly at first, then faster, until I'm panting and whimpering. His hands squeeze my ass, pulling me in closer so that there's just the right amount of pressure on my clit from his pelvis. No doubt about it, the man knows exactly what I need.

"Close," I warn as he impales me harder, deeper, faster. "So … so … so…" I grit my teeth as the sparks ignite the flame and set off the detonation. "Oh, God!"

I come in a rush of shudders as the electric current slays me. Another mini orgasm is triggered when Kingston finds his release, driving into me one final time as he growls my name against my neck.

I focus on breathing as he sets me on my feet. My knees are weak, my thighs trembling, but I manage to use the wall at my back to keep me upright.

"Better?" he asks, his forehead pressed to mine, his breaths labored from his efforts.

"So much better," I admit because it's true. Now that he's quite literally fucked some of my anxiety out of me, I feel like can accomplish anything.

Yep. That definitely worked as a distraction.

Two hours later…

KINGSTON

"Welcome," I greet as I open the front door and smile, genuinely happy to see the friends and family who are descending for this holiday.

Perhaps it was the sex in the shower or maybe just the fact that I've got the day off, but I'm feeling better than I have in a while. Lighter, I think.

Standing on my front porch, donning their Texas winter wear—long sleeves, jeans, lightweight coats—and huge smiles are my brother-in-law Spencer, his wife, Noelle, and their daughter.

My niece is already hopping up and down, eager for my attention.

"I'm sorry, is there something going on"—I gesture in a circular swiping motion in Lotus's direction while looking at Spencer—"down here?"

"Uncle Goalie," she says firmly with the kind of sass only a three-year-old can muster.

I jerk my attention downward and widen my eyes. "Oh, hey, little flower. I didn't see you there."

Lotus plants her hands on her hips. "My name's Lotus, not little flower."

"Oh. My bad. Hey, Lotus. How are you?"

Her smile is as bright as the sunshine. Clearly she doesn't feel the need to tell me how she is, because she responds with, "Where's Cason?"

"He's upstairs waiting for you."

Lotus spins to face her parents. "Can I go upstairs? Pretty please?"

"Of course," Noelle answers. "Just remember, you and Cason have to clean up before we leave."

"Okay!" she calls out, already heading for the stairs.

"Ellie's in the kitchen," I tell Noelle as I help her out of her coat and place it on the rack Ellie bought specifically for when guests come over.

"I hope there's wine," she announces, making a beeline for her best friend, her hand protectively covering her baby bump.

"You can't have wine," Spencer reminds her.

Noelle exhales heavily. "A girl can dream, can't she?"

"She's ready to have the baby," Spencer informs me with a dramatic sigh. "And to think she's got three more months to go."

I laugh. "Well, if it's any consolation, Ellie promised not to drink wine in front of her." I don't bother telling him how much she's already had to drink.

"And we both know how well that'll work."

Yes, we do. Ellie promises but rarely does she ever follow through. Mostly because Noelle gives her crap about it until she can't help herself.

"How're things?" I ask Spencer as the man hangs up his own coat.

"Can't complain. Got the day off and all."

I chuckle. "I was just thinking the same thing."

Although Spencer and I both tossed around the idea of retiring from the NHL a few years back, we changed our tunes shortly after our kids were born. Being new fathers obviously changed us nearly four years ago, and I can't say I am disappointed in my decision. The team is well on its way to winning another Stanley Cup this year—it would be the second time in four years—and I am grateful to be a part of it.

"Wanna beer?" I offer.

"Won't turn it down. Anyone else here?"

"Scott's in the game room watching the Cowboys." My brother is a huge fan, and I know without a doubt someone will give him shit about it today just for the sake of it. Doesn't matter that the Dallas Cowboys are kicking ass and taking names this year.

"Of course he is," Spencer laughs.

"James and Amber are helping Ellie with the final touches in the kitchen. Bianca's upstairs, probably primping in front of the mirror."

I lead the way to the wet bar in the downstairs media room, where I keep beer in the small refrigerator. It's not that I am avoiding the kitchen... Okay, yes, I am avoiding the kitchen. I know my wife is currently fretting over the fact Bianca's boyfriend is on the way, and now that Noelle is here, I'm sure it's only getting more dramatic.

"Oh, and Heath's on his way."

Spencer stops and turns his full attention on me. "I thought he had other plans for Thanksgiving."

"Changed his mind," I say with a frown, passing over one of the bottles after I open it. "That a problem?"

"Julie's coming," he says, as though mentioning Noelle's sister should make a lightbulb go off in my head.

"I know," I tell him. No way would Ellie leave out Noelle's sister from Thanksgiving. Even Noelle's parents are coming for the festivities. We are a close bunch.

"Shit."

I frown. "What's wrong?"

Spencer instantly shakes his head. "Nothing. Never mind."

I grab his arm and halt him from walking away. "What don't I know?"

"Let's just say, having Bianca's boyfriend at the dining table probably won't be the most dramatic event of the evening."

I stare at him, not sure what that means but more than a little worried to find out.

ELLIE

Thanks to James and Amber, I've got most of the dinner preparations completed. As soon as Noelle arrived, she inserted herself in the middle of it, insisting she be allowed to help, so I gave her a few tasks to complete just to keep her out from under my feet. Well, that and because I'm sneaking wine despite my promise to her that I won't drink. It's been a rough day. Sue me.

Just when the wine is starting to ease some of my tension, Noelle's parents and her sister arrive, the three of them greeting me in the kitchen, where I'm still attempting to work. Thankfully, Noelle is here to keep them somewhat occupied, which allows me to direct Amber as to how to set the table. As soon as my directions are complete, I hear a shocked huff, drawing my attention across the way. It takes a second for me to replay what I said, and as soon as I do, I grimace.

I think it's safe to say that I am the queen of dysfunctional get-togethers.

All this time, I have been anxious about my daughter's boyfriend coming to dinner, and I never even stopped to consider the fact that my brother-in-law and Noelle's sister are about to be under the same roof for the first time since—

"I cannot believe you didn't tell me he was coming," Julie snaps at Noelle.

"I didn't know," she declares, hands on her hips, her cute pregnancy belly softening her attempt at frustration.

"It's true," I chime in. "Heath originally declined our invitation."

Julie takes a deep breath and downs what's left of her wine before snagging my glass and gulping it, too.

I don't know the gory details of what caused her complete dislike for Kingston's brother, but I have a feeling it has something to do with a one-night stand neither of them will cop to. I remember the two of them making eyes at each other during a team event, and later that night, I lost track of them both for a short time.

Not that I try to keep up with Heath's conquests. The man is a playboy of the highest order, shown up by only one other member on the team—Patrick Benne—who I would go so far as to say is a man-whore.

But hey, they are all grown-ups, and it sucks that I have to remind them of that fact now that we are about to sit down to dinner.

"Can we wait a few more minutes, Mom?" Bianca pleads, joining us in the kitchen. "Trevor is on his way."

I nod and she hurries out of the room, clearly not wanting to get in the middle of this.

I can't blame her. I want to sneak out myself, and I probably would if it wasn't for the fact that I am the one responsible for dinner this year. Why I volunteered to cook Thanksgiving dinner, I will never know.

"The table's set. What else can I help with?" Amber asks, returning from the dining room.

I peer over at Bianca's stepmother and smile. "I think we're about ready for the food, but Bianca wants us to wait a few more minutes."

She smiles and nods. "This is going to be interesting."

That is probably an understatement. When James and Amber arrived to help out, I instantly began interrogating Bianca's father about this Trevor boy. Turns out, Bianca hasn't introduced them to him either. Unlike me, though, they don't seem at all worried about it.

Truth is, I probably wouldn't be so up in arms if I could just relax and enjoy another glass of wine, but thanks to my promise to my pregnant best friend, I'm having to sneak around while pretending to boycott wine for her benefit.

What was I thinking?

Twenty minutes later, I go in search of Bianca, finding my daughter sitting on the couch in the darkened formal living room, her eyes glued to her phone. There's no mistaking the droop of her shoulders.

"What's wrong?" I ask softly.

Her gaze slides up to me. "I don't think he's coming."

"Why would you say that?"

"Because he hasn't messaged me back."

"But he told you he was on the way?"

"Not exactly."

Ah.

"Do you want me to call him?" I offer, knowing full well what my daughter will say before she says it.

"God, no."

I smile to myself. "I will if you need me to. I will call him up and tell him to march his butt right on over here."

Bianca chuckles, like I hoped she would. "Mom."

"What? I ain't scared of no boy."

She laughs a little more but there's still too much tension in her shoulders.

"Better yet, I'll have Rush call him. Or Spencer."

Bianca huffs a laugh.

I can tell she's trying not to let her boyfriend's absence drag her down, but clearly she's upset by it. Which is why I am willing to call him up and give him a piece of my mind.

"Well, why don't you come in here with us, so we——"

I don't get the full sentence out when her phone buzzes in her hand. Bianca's gaze slams into the device, and then she's shooting to her feet like her ass is on a spring.

"He's here," she says with more enthusiasm than I've seen her have in years.

"Go answer the door," I tell her a second before the doorbell rings. "If you don't——"

Unfortunately, she doesn't get there fast enough.

***

KINGSTON

It's a fluke that I'm walking by the front door when the doorbell rings.

It's happenstance that Spencer is walking beside me.

However, I intentionally wave over Heath and Scott, my two hockey-playing brothers, to help out. Not with answering the door, because I'm an adult, I can do that myself, but I do need some help greeting Bianca's boyfriend.

The four of us make a wall as I open the front door to greet the boy who nearly had my stepdaughter in tears a few minutes ago.

"Who're you?" I demand, ensuring my tone is rough as I let the door swing wide.

The young man is dressed in a pair of khakis and a sweater, looking every bit the seventeen-year-old I assume him to be. His eyes widen as he takes us all in.

"Trevor," he says, the word trembling on his lips.

"Trevor who?" Scott demands.

"Uh … Trevor McCord?"

"Is that a question or a statement?" Heath chimes in.

"A statement?" the boy says.

"Are you sure about that?" Spencer adds.

Trevor, clearly realizing we aren't going to let up, changes course. "Is … uh … Bianca home?"

"Depends," I tell him. "What do you want with her?"

"I … um…"

"Spit it out, boy," Spencer barks.

"Uncle Spencer," Bianca snaps from behind us. "You better be nice."

Spencer glances at me, smirks. "I'm always nice. I was just saying hello to your little friend. I think he's cold standing outside. He's shivering."

I laugh. The boy isn't shivering, he's trembling. As in, he's scared, not cold.

"Let him come in," Bianca insists.

"Don't touch anything," I warn the boy with a glare.

"Yes, sir."

"You stop it," my wife says, shoving me aside so Trevor can come into the house. "Hello, Trevor. I'm Ellie, Bianca's mom. These overgrown boys are hockey players. Just ignore them."

Trevor steps inside, his full attention on my wife as though she might possibly be able to save him from us.

I hear Trevor speak, but his words are muffled, his nervousness obvious. Can you really blame him? I wouldn't want to meet anyone's parents on Thanksgiving or any holiday for that matter. And I certainly wouldn't want to come toe to toe with four hockey players at the girlfriend's house.

"Why don't you two have a seat in the kitchen," Ellie tells Bianca. "Away from the bullies."

I watch my stepdaughter, the way her eyes light up with relief.

"I think I'll eat in the kitchen, too," Heath calls out behind them.

Ellie rounds on him. "No, you certainly will not."

I see Heath's surprise but I don't say a word, enjoying the moment.

"You are going to go into the dining room, sit down, and be on your best behavior. If you don't have anything nice to say, don't say anything at all."

"What did I do?" Heath asks, clearly surprised.

"I have no idea," she tells him. "Nor do I want to know." Ellie's eyes meet mine briefly then shift back to Heath. "And for the record, I told Julie the same thing. Don't make me separate you two."

Yep, that's my wife. The woman everyone likes.

As for why they like her ... well, sometimes I think it's because she scares the shit out of them.

The good news is, she managed to keep everyone in line throughout the evening. The bad news is, I think she drank all the wine.

Holiday Road Trip

Grant, Lane, and Grace from *Betting on Grace*

Grant and Lane surprise Grace with a holiday road trip. See how they kick off their long weekend.

Friday, November 26, 2021

GRACE LAMBERT TRAVERSED THE FINAL STEP TO the main floor, her gaze swinging around in an effort to locate her sister. Trinity, Faith, Mercy, Hope. Any one of them would work; it didn't matter who.

"Hey!" she called out, hoping someone was paying attention. "Room four needs to be cleaned."

She walked through the entertainment room, the dining room, peeked in the kitchen, found no one.

No guests, no employees, and no sisters.

Grace marched to the back door, pushing the screen open so hard it hit the house before rebounding. Thankfully, she was out of the way and down the steps to the—

"What is this?" she demanded, talking to no one because there was no one out here, either.

However, while there were no people lurking, there was what looked to be a forty-foot-long fifth wheel travel trailer parked where it shouldn't be.

"Who left this here?" she shouted, hoping to draw someone's attention.

Where the hell was everyone?

She headed around to find an entrance to the RV that was currently hitched to what suspiciously looked like Lane's Ram 2500.

"Lane Miller! Why is—"

Her tirade was cut off when Lane Miller and Grant Kingsley—the men she loved and had pledged her life to— appeared, both grinning from ear to ear. Those grins ... they were mischievous and, if she wasn't mistaken, had more than a little pride mixed in.

"What are you two up to?"

Lane was the first to speak, his handsome face still smiling. "Nothin', darlin'. Just, you know, packin' for a trip."

Grace narrowed her eyes. "A trip? And where do you think you're goin'?"

"We," Grant corrected. "*We* are goin'."

Yep, they were definitely up to something.

She looked from one to the other. "You do know this is a holiday."

"Technically, *yesterday* was a holiday," Grant stated. "Thanksgiving is officially behind us."

She canted her head, as though willing him to understand. "Which makes today Black Friday."

"Not a holiday, just a conspiracy created by retailers to rake in the dough," Grant said with a laugh. "No one's expecting us for Black Friday dinner."

He had a point.

Confusion, and perhaps an inkling of excitement, settled around her. "So where do you think *we* are goin'?"

"Not too far, but the three of us are gettin' away for the weekend."

"The weekend. It's Friday mornin'." Which meant they had chores to complete, guests to tend to, animals to take care of.

"Okay, so it's a long weekend," Grant corrected with a smirk.

"What about the chores?"

"Main ones are done," he said easily.

Grace cocked an eyebrow. "And when do we supposedly leave?"

"As soon as you get that pretty ass in the truck," Lane said, moving closer.

She turned to cast a skeptical look at the RV. "First of all, if I agreed to a surprise long-weekend trip, I would have to pack."

"Already done for you," Lane noted.

She should've known he was going to say that.

"Secondly, if I agreed, I would have to tell my sisters and okay it with my father."

"Done and done," Grant supplied.

Grace wasn't sure she believed this was real. Maybe she was dreaming because seriously? A long weekend? She couldn't remember the last time they'd ventured away from Dead Heat Ranch, much less gone away for an extended period of time. There was so much going on these days what with people wanting to get away from the hustle and bustle, trying to find a place to hide out for a little while. They'd anticipated going belly up when Covid hit, but it turned out their little dude ranch getaway offered the perfect opportunity for people to put some distance between themselves.

Of course, that meant they were up to their eyeballs in chores, which left very little time for themselves.

Lane gave a long, sweeping gesture toward the truck. "Your chariot awaits, m'lady."

She chuckled, glancing over at Grant. "Are you sure my father knows?"

"Knows and approves." The confidence in his tone told her he wasn't lying.

Grace looked between her men again, studying their faces in an attempt to ensure this wasn't some sort of trick.

It was in her nature to argue, but she couldn't find it in her to do so. Who was she to turn down a weekend getaway? Even the thought of spending it in an RV wasn't a bad one. Anything for just a few days of R and R.

"Come on," Grant said, nodding toward the truck. "Let's hit the road. I'd like to be set up by nightfall."

"Nightfall?"

Rather than answer her, Grant reached out and took her arm, steering her toward the truck. He opened the back door for her, but she stepped around him and climbed into the front.

"I told you she'd do that," Lane said with a laugh as he climbed in the driver's seat.

———

GRANT COULDN'T REMEMBER THE LAST TIME THE three of them had been alone, much less away from the ranch they called home. This time of year especially, the ranch was booming, guests coming and going, wanting to get in a little bit of fun during the winter break. Since they rarely saw weather bad enough to shut things down, Dead Heat Ranch was always open for business, and the tourists looking to get their hands dirty on a working dude ranch seemed endless.

So, yes, this little excursion had required some finesse, but Grant had come up with the idea in late August, filling Lane in on it and getting his support. From there, they'd worked hard to keep it a secret from Gracie, which wasn't an easy feat.

But now they were here, and the weekend was laid out before them: sleeping in, making s'mores by the campfire, and grabbing a nature hike here and there. Those were all items on his to-do list.

And sex. He definitely couldn't forget that one. In fact, it was a priority as far as he was concerned because there never seemed enough time in the day for the three of them to come together appropriately. A few stolen moments every so often wasn't what Grant considered quality time.

While Lane worked to get the fifth wheel trailer leveled out so they could disconnect from the truck, Grant headed around to get the hookups in place.

"Put me to work, boss," Gracie insisted as she ambled around the trailer. "I need somethin' to do."

Grant smirked, focused on his task. "I can think of somethin' you can do."

She laughed. "Yeah? Here? Now?"

Grant's gaze snapped to her face, and he saw the woman he loved more than life staring down at his now thickening cock. Sure, it was concealed behind the zipper of his jeans, but the denim was doing little to restrain the damn thing.

"Gracie," he warned.

"What? Can't blame a girl for tryin'."

No, he couldn't blame his feisty cowgirl considering she was a handful and always had been. In fact, Grant had been looking forward to this getaway for a while now and wouldn't mind a single bit if they spent every possible minute of it naked.

"All set," Lane hollered from the front of the trailer.

When Grant heard the truck's diesel engine start up as Lane pulled it away from the RV, he got the hookups in place.

Fifteen minutes later, they were up and running.

"Do I get to see this thing anytime soon? Or is it some sorta secret hideout and I have to figure out the password?" Gracie asked, hands on her hips as she stared at him.

"Hmm." Grant stepped toward her, gripped her hips, and pulled her into him. "I like that idea. Every guess you get wrong, you can remove an article of clothing."

Gracie's eyebrows arched. "It can be arranged, cowboy. Or … you could just let me see inside and I can strip it all off at once."

"I bet we could arrange that." Grant grinned, taking her hand and leading her around to the main door.

It was already unlocked and he could hear Lane rummaging around inside.

"Go on. See it for yourself."

Grant followed Gracie inside, then shut and locked the door behind them. Lane shot him a smirk, then turned his attention to Gracie as she surveyed the space.

"This is fantastic," she said with a wondrous exhale.

It wasn't the top of the line, by any means, but it was brand-new and more than adequate with the single bedroom, full kitchen, dinette, and enormous living room. It had taken him and Lane more than one trip to various dealerships before they were finally in agreement on which one they wanted. Because they intended to utilize the RV every chance they could, they'd decided it needed to have the creature comforts necessary to allow for an enjoyable weekend here and there. This one had everything they could possibly need and then some.

"Check out the bedroom," Lane encouraged, motioning toward the back of the trailer.

Gracie didn't hesitate, and Lane fell in right behind her. Grant followed suit.

"This is impressive, except—"

Lane pressed a button and the slide in the bedroom started to expand, adding additional space as the bed shifted outward.

Gracie laughed. "Yep. That does it."

"I think our first order of business is to test out the bed," Lane said, stepping up behind Gracie.

"I might be game, but someone's gonna have to turn some heat on in here."

Grant hated to leave them for a second, but he agreed. The RV was a bit chilly, which made getting naked not so appealing.

When he returned to the bedroom, he found Gracie and Lane already on the bed, Lane's big body covering her almost completely. Grant couldn't help it, he watched from the doorway, admiring the way the two of them moved together. He knew he would never tire of watching them. They were hot as hell, and seeing them like that never ceased to raise his blood pressure.

"You better not tease me," Gracie warned. "I know you, Lane Miller. You like to get me all hot and bothered and then run out. It ain't gonna be funny this time."

Lane lifted his head and grinned. "I ain't goin' nowhere."

Grant laughed because he'd been on the receiving end of that joke a time or two. He'd also dealt it back to Lane a couple of times, which he'd learned was a hell of a lot harder than he'd expected it to be.

"You can prove it by strippin' first," Grant told him, stepping into the room.

Lane's head turned and he looked at Grant with a smirk on his handsome face.

LANE WAS NOT A MAN WHO SHIED away from getting naked, and he damn sure wasn't about to start now.

When Grant cocked an eyebrow, obviously daring him to strip, Lane went up to his knees and began unbuttoning his shirt. Beneath him, Gracie put her hands behind her head and watched him as though he was her favorite TV show.

Once his button-down was off, he reached behind his head and gripped the T-shirt, pulling it off in one easy move and tossing it to the floor. He was watching Gracie as he did because he wanted to see the sparkle in her eye when she looked at his chest. They'd been together for years, and yet every time he took off his shirt, his sexy woman got a gleam in her eye that made his cock stand up and take notice.

"Mmm," she said, her gaze caressing over the planes of his chest.

"You like?"

"I think you get hotter every day," she said approvingly before looking at Grant. "Your turn."

"You think you're directing this show?" Grant asked, a chuckle following.

"I think I am, yes," she answered, her voice raspier than when they'd come inside.

Gracie moved one hand enough to flutter her fingers in a *go ahead, get on with it* motion.

Lane turned his head, watched as Grant took another step into the room even as he was quickly shedding his coat and then pulling his long-sleeve Henley over his head.

"Very, very nice," Gracie said, her appreciation genuine. "Now what're you boys gonna do?"

Another dare, one Lane had gotten familiar with over the years. It hadn't taken much for them to realize that Gracie enjoyed watching the two of them together. Not that Lane needed an audience to touch the man he craved more than air, but knowing she was watching made it that much hotter.

Lane didn't move, but he didn't have to because Grant came up behind him, his work-rough hands sliding over his shoulders and then down his chest. Just the light brush of his skin was enough for Lane's cock to swell. He fucking loved when they touched him. Loved it.

"This what you want?" Grant taunted her.

Lane saw the sparkle in her eyes as she followed Grant's hands where they moved over his chest.

"I think you're gonna have to pitch in here, darlin'," Lane said, reaching for the buckle on his belt.

"Yeah?" She grinned, hands still behind her head as though she didn't have a care in the world.

"Yeah." Lane leaned into Grant, enjoying the feel of his hands on his chest. He tried to focus on unbuckling his belt, but it took effort. The heat of Grant's body never failed to distract him.

Somehow he managed to free his cock, the damn thing pulsing in his grip as he watched Gracie watching him.

"Your mouth, Gracie," he rasped, inhaling sharply when Grant pinched his nipples. "Put your mouth on me."

The blasted woman licked her lips but remained where she was.

"You don't, I will," Grant taunted her.

That got her attention because, like him, Gracie never backed down from a challenge either.

She rolled to her knees and crawled toward him on all fours, her eyes glittering with desire and amusement. And then her mouth was on him, and the only thing Lane could do was inhale and exhale because, blessed mother of all things, her mouth was heaven. Soft and warm and—

"Fuck, yes, Gracie," he whispered, brushing his hand over her head as she licked and sucked him.

Grant urged Lane to lift up, which he managed to do without dislodging from Gracie's perfect mouth. Somehow, Grant managed to remove his boots, then strip his jeans down his legs, all while Gracie sucked his dick with a skill and precision she'd mastered over the years. She focused on him as though her only goal was to make him lose his mind, and it worked because she knew exactly what he wanted and she didn't hesitate to give it.

"Her turn," Grant grumbled, nudging Lane forward.

"Ah, Gracie," Lane mumbled, pumping his hips despite his desire to hold off. "You gotta slow down, baby."

She sucked him harder, a bolt of painful pleasure ricocheting up his spine.

Ah, hell. He wasn't ready to come yet, but she was making it nearly impossible to refrain. She was too good at that.

It took effort, but Lane managed to dislodge from her mouth. As soon as he was free, he grabbed her and rolled them so that he was flat on his back and she was draping him like a blanket. She giggled when Grant went for her feet, tugging her boots off, one then the other.

Lane took advantage, melding his mouth to hers.

God, he loved this woman. He loved her so much, every time he looked at her, he felt it in his chest. She was their everything. Laughter and love, peace and joy, anger and passion. He loved every part of her.

"I want you inside me," Gracie mumbled against his lips.

Especially the naughty parts.

THERE WAS NOTHING GRACE ENJOYED MORE THAN watching Grant and Lane together.

Admittedly, she'd been taken aback in the beginning when she learned that they were intimate. It had shocked her to the toes of her boots, and she certainly hadn't expected to find it so damn erotic.

Yet here they were, all these years later and she couldn't get enough of watching them together. Two sinfully hot cowboys, their bodies honed from endless days of hard, back-breaking work. She could've spent a lifetime watching and she'd never get enough of them.

Participating was a good thing, too, sure. She definitely enjoyed being the filling in this hot man sandwich, but Grace wasn't selfish. Often.

"Lane…" Grace ground her hips against him, wishing he would fill the empty ache within her.

Rather than give in to her pleas, Lane waited until Grant had stripped her naked before he easily maneuvered her so that she was straddling his face.

Not exactly what she'd been angling for, but hell, she wasn't going to complain. The man's tongue belonged in a class of its own.

"This is what I'm talkin' about," Lane mumbled, his fingertips pressing into her hips as he pulled her pussy closer to his mouth.

Grace had just enough time to slam her palm flat on the outer wall of the RV as Lane flicked her clit with the tip of his tongue. Electricity jolted her insides as pleasure detonated.

"Ride my face, baby," he growled, his big hands cupping her ass and pulling her flush to his face.

Grace couldn't resist. It felt too good. The way he alternated between licking, flicking, and fucking her with his magnificent tongue. It wasn't long before she was pressing against him, increasing the friction on her clit.

He moaned against her, the vibrations causing goose bumps to form on her arms as she chased the release that was just out of reach.

Groaning, Grace pressed her palm to the wall and her hips down as she ground herself on his mouth.

"Oh, God … oh, God … Oh!" Grace threw her head back as lightning slammed through her entire body, radiating through every nerve ending as a cataclysmic orgasm pummeled her.

Falling off of Lane, Grace fought to catch her breath even as she mumbled, "I need more."

"What's that?"

She glanced over at Grant. "Fuck me," she bit out. "I need one or both of you to fuck me. Now."

His smile was devilish and it made her insides tighten.

"Both of us?"

Grace nodded, loving the way his eyes flashed with heat. She absolutely loved when they fucked her at the same time, one buried in her pussy, the other in her ass. Before them, she'd had no idea she could even enjoy anal sex, much less double penetration, but it turned out she craved it like a drug. Nothing else made her feel quite so complete as being sandwiched between them, having them inside her at the same time.

Lane was the first to move, rolling over and settling his hips between her thighs. Grace stared at his handsome face as his thick cock pressed against her opening.

"You ready for me, baby?"

"Always," she said, digging her heel into his ass and urging him inside her.

His groan was heavenly as his eyes rolled back, his cock stretching her as he pressed his hips forward.

"God, yes," she moaned, gripping his biceps. "Fuck me, Lane."

"You can't come yet," he warned.

Grace shook her head. "I won't, I promise."

It was a lie. She couldn't promise anything. When it came to orgasms, she damn sure had no intention of holding off.

Lane pulled out slowly, met her gaze, held it, and his smile was the only warning she received before he slammed into her.

Chills raced down her spine, the sensation so delicious it was a wonder she didn't explode.

And then he was moving, his hips pounding into her, the bed rocking from the momentum. She hissed and whimpered, letting the pleasure overwhelm her.

"My turn."

The deep boom of Grant's voice brought Lane's hips to a stop, and Grace groaned her frustration, which got a laugh in return.

With one easy move, Lane rolled to his back, taking her with him, never dislodging from within her.

It was her turn to smile, because in this position, she was in control.

At least, she'd thought she was, but she hadn't realized Lane's knees were bent, his feet on the floor, and Grant was already stepping up behind her.

"Relax, baby," Lane said, pulling her mouth down to his. "Let us do all the work."

She nipped his lip and grunted, giving in when she felt the press of Grant's cock against her back hole.

Clearly Grant was as eager as she was, because he didn't tease or torment, merely pressed forward, sliding his lube-slick cock past the tight ring of muscles.

"Oh, God, yes," she moaned, pressing her chest to Lane's and relaxing to ease the initial discomfort.

And then they were fucking her. Grant in her ass, Lane in her pussy, both men working in tandem to bring her the most pleasure. She let herself go, giving in to the sensations that washed over her, consuming her entire being. She didn't know how to describe the feeling of being filled by two men at one time, much less when it was two men she loved beyond measure. It was more than merely sex, more than intimacy, it was—

"Grant! Lane!" The first orgasm obliterated her mind, leaving her a boneless heap as they plied her with more pleasure.

"Come for us again, baby," Grant urged, his hands gripping her hips.

It wasn't long before another orgasm rocked her, this one draining more of her energy.

"You ready?"

Grace wasn't sure who Grant was speaking to, but she couldn't form an answer even if she wanted to. Another orgasm was cresting as the friction built.

"Fuck, yes," Lane crooned.

Grace sucked in air when someone's hand snaked between her body and Lane's, deft fingers finding her clit.

They slammed into her and the pressure built again, combined with the press of those glorious fingers on her clit. Grace cried out, every muscle locking as the mother of all orgasms stole her breath and a little more of her soul.

A second later, her men came, both shouting her name as they filled her.

"DOES THIS MEAN A NAP'S IN ORDER?"

Grant peered over at Gracie, pressed a kiss to her forehead. "If that's what you want."

Although the three of them had fallen into a heap on the bed after that round, Grant wasn't quite ready to fall asleep, but he certainly wouldn't fault Gracie for it. She deserved some rest considering the amount of work she put in on the ranch. It took a tremendous amount of effort to keep Dead Heat Ranch running smoothly, and Gracie and her sisters did whatever it took to help out.

"Maybe not a nap," she said, stretching. "But I wouldn't complain about lunch."

"That can be arranged," Lane said as he shifted out from under Gracie and onto his feet. "You two can clean up, I'll start on some sandwiches."

"Grilled cheese," Gracie said on a pleased groan. "Pretty please."

Lane chuckled, rolling to a sitting position. "Fine. Grilled cheese for our lady."

"I get the shower first!" she announced, scurrying out of the bed as though Grant was going to race her.

He probably should have, but he couldn't seem to get his muscles on board. Right now, he was content in this space, with these people.

"One or two?" Lane offered.

"Two," he answered easily. "Want some help?"

"Nah. I'll holler when it's ready."

Grant nodded, watched as Lane pulled on his jeans, covering that perfectly contoured ass. Yeah, it was a shame for the man to cover himself up.

When Lane slipped out of the room, Grant remained where he was, listened as Gracie freshened up in the small bathroom. When she came out, joining Lane in the kitchen, he forced himself to his feet. After a quick shower in the ridiculously small enclosure with as little water as he could manage, he got dressed and joined them.

"I left a couple on the counter," Lane said from his spot at the small dinette table.

"What's next on the agenda?" Gracie asked.

"First, we eat."

"Already done," she said quickly, her fingers drumming on the table as though her patience was waning.

"I coulda sworn we fucked some of that energy outta her," Lane joked. "Maybe another round's what you need."

"Maybe."

Grant cut a sideways glance at Gracie. The woman was awfully feisty. Had been for a few weeks now and he wondered what had gotten into her.

Not that he minded being used as a stud whenever she needed. He would sign up for that task any day of the week.

"Relax," Grant told her. "We've got time."

"We've got the whole weekend," Lane added.

Gracie peered between the two of them, exhaled dramatically. "Fine."

Yep, this was exactly what they needed.

Three days in the woods, alone. Together.

Now *that* should be a day to celebrate.

Naughty Cruise

Landon, Langston, and Luci from *Office Intrigue Duet*

See how quickly things heat up when Master and Sir take their submissive Luci on a naughty cruise.

Thursday, December 9, 2021

LUCI

I wish I could've said that a naughty sex cruise was something I'd considered a possibility early on in my relationship with Landon and Langston Moore, but I would be lying. And that was saying something considering all that I'd learned in the years we'd been together. It all began when they hired me to work for Chatter PR, the public relations firm they started with two other partners. Since then, Master and Sir have taught me so much about myself, about my needs, desires, and most importantly, about love.

We live a full-time Dominant/submissive lifestyle. At home, at work, at play. I am their pet twenty-four/seven. Yes, we are members of a BDSM club, and we go there frequently, enjoying everything the place has to offer. Namely, I enjoy everything my two Dominants have to offer me. But the truth is, when they surprised me with a naughty cruise for the holidays, I initially thought they were joking.

They weren't and we were now onboard the enormous ship alongside a few hundred others who were here to enjoy the kinky festivities.

"Didn't you say Addison and Clarissa would be here?" I prompted as Master (Langston) led the way to our cabin.

"They are," he confirmed, his gaze sliding over me and a smile forming. "You're not nervous, are you?"

Of course I wasn't nervous.

Okay, that was a huge lie. I was nervous. I never knew what Master and Sir had in store for me. They enjoyed pushing my boundaries to their limits, and though I welcomed the challenge, enjoyed it even, I still got a flutter in my belly thinking about what they might do next.

Master chuckled softly as he stopped at one of the doors.

I waited patiently for him to unlock it, then preceded him into the room when he gestured for me to go. I wasn't but a few feet inside when I stopped, realizing this wasn't an ordinary cabin. I had envisioned something small, maybe with a king-sized bed (if we were lucky) crowded by walls with a single porthole above it.

Nope.

This was not that.

In fact, this was very much like some of the hotel rooms we'd stayed in over the years. Open, airy. Comfortable. The only difference was that everything in the room was secured, likely a safety precaution because we would be on the open sea.

It was absolutely lovely. But the best part? Well, that would be the balcony that overlooked the water.

"Holy crap," I shrieked, moving deeper into the space and fighting the urge to skip.

Planting my hands on the glass, I stared out at the expanse of water beyond. It was beautiful. I'd never been on a cruise before, wasn't sure I'd ever cared to go, but now that I was here, I wanted to enjoy all that it had to offer.

"I take it you approve?"

I turned back to survey the room, ignoring his jab.

"It's okay," I said with a shrug. "If it was all they had, I guess."

He laughed, a sexy sound that made my skin tingle. I loved to hear this man laugh, and considering he hadn't done much of it when I first met him, I'd say we'd come a long, *long* way.

Some might say Langston and Landon Moore were interchangeable considering how similar they were. For starters, they were identical twins, although time and age had shifted their appearance enough to tell the difference between them. And two, their personalities were vastly different. Langston, who I referred to only as Master, was the more rigid, rule-abiding twin. He enjoyed punishing me for any and all reasons. And Landon, who I called Sir, was more laid-back, more ... *comforting*, if you would.

And because of their differences as well as their similarities, I loved them wholeheartedly, and I had pledged my love and my submission to both of them for eternity.

Before I could think to dodge, Master grabbed me up and tossed me onto the enormous bed with its many pillows and downy-soft comforter.

"Uh-uh," he growled, gripping my ankles before I could scoot away from him. "Stay right there."

God, I loved when he got that gravelly rasp to his voice. It was a signal that he was going to devour me whole, and since they'd purposely made me wait for the past week, it was only fair that he was eager for the games to begin. I certainly was.

I stilled, staring up at the man I loved more than life itself. To be fair, there were two men I loved more than life, but for the moment, Master was here while Sir was taking care of something. He wouldn't tell me what, but I was almost certain it was going to be something I would enjoy in the long run.

"You have five minutes," Master informed me, standing at the side of the bed and staring down at me with a grin. "Get your questions out now, because when your time is up, you're no longer allowed to ask any more."

"For the whole trip?" I inquired, genuinely curious as to whether we were going to be following high protocol.

"While in the presence of a Dom, yes. That includes me and Landon."

His words sent a frisson of heat through my entire being. It had been a while since he'd gone full Dom on me. I'd been looking forward to this trip for a while now, eager to submit to him and Sir fully. Due to busy schedules, we'd gotten a bit lax in our lifestyle. Which ultimately meant they didn't hold me as accountable for my actions as they should. That, plus we hadn't had much time to play, and I knew they needed this as much as I did.

"Are there rules?" I asked as Master's big, warm hands gripped my ankles and began a slow glide up my shins to my knees.

"Strict rules, yes," he confirmed. "You will have plenty of time to enjoy yourself, just be mindful of who's around you at all times."

Meaning if there was a Dominant in my presence, I was to be respectful.

He gripped my knees. "And we will conform to high protocol during some of the festivities."

Meaning I would not be allowed to do anything without their direction.

"What about clothes? Do I get to wear them?"

His hazel eyes shifted to my face. "Unless I say otherwise."

I smiled. "And will you? Say otherwise?"

"What do you think?"

I figured if I was allowed to be dressed at all, I would be lucky. I'd long ago learned that my Dominants preferred me to be naked. At home, it was a frequent occurrence. Not so much in the office anymore, but there were days when Master or Sir would have me strip for one reason or another. Sometimes even when there were others there, depending on what I'd done or the mood they were in.

While many didn't understand our sexual proclivities, I'd long ago stopped trying to pretend I was something I wasn't. This was my life and I loved it, and while I enjoyed being a bratty little submissive on occasion, Master and Sir knew I was committed to them fully: heart, body, and soul.

"Are there rules for the Dominants?" I asked, letting my legs fall open when Master urged my knees apart.

"Meaning?"

"Do I take commands from other Dominants?"

"No." His eyes darkened. "There are no singles on this cruise. Dominants or submissives. You're only to take instruction and punishment from us."

I loved how he tacked on punishment as though it was a forgone conclusion. Then again, I guess it was. I couldn't recall a single week that had gone by when I hadn't been punished in one way or another. Granted, I often pushed them to the point of no return, so I earned every delectable second.

"One minute," Master said, his attention returning to between my legs as he lifted the skirt I was wearing.

Cool air caressed my bare pussy and I inhaled sharply as a bolt of need lanced me.

"Will I…" My question died off on a moan as Langston's thumbs parted my labia.

"Thirty seconds," he noted, massaging my lower lips.

"Never mind," I mumbled, closing my eyes and giving myself over to the exquisite sensation.

"Time," Master growled.

For a brief moment, his touch fell away, but it returned when he smacked my pussy with the flat of his hand.

I cried out as glorious sensation shot through me, a delectable mixture of pain and pleasure.

"For the next seven days, this body is ours to do with as we please," Master stated firmly, his Dom voice in full force. "What's your safe word?"

"I don't need one, Master, but I'll use *red* in the event there's a problem."

"Good girl."

I smiled to myself. *Let the games begin.*

MASTER
(Langston)

If Luci thought I didn't notice the smirk on her face, she was sadly mistaken. In fact, I caught every nuance of her expression because I was always paying attention. I figured it had something to do with our lifestyle and the intensity of it at times. I was usually watching to ensure she was all right considering the drastic things we were known to have her do.

So, yes, I noticed the smile. I knew she'd been looking forward to this cruise since the day my brother mentioned it to her. It wasn't something I would've signed up for before she came into our lives, but these days I was doing quite a lot of things that weren't normal for me. I didn't mind. Certainly not if it made her happy.

"Don't move," I commanded Luci again, leaving her pussy splayed for my viewing pleasure.

"Yes, Master," she said softly, acknowledging the fact her free time was over and that, going forward, everything she did would be for my pleasure. Mine and Landon's.

She was quite a sight, I wouldn't lie. Her pussy bare, legs spread, hair fanned out on the bed.

I left her like that and headed for the wardrobe to find an outfit for this afternoon's event.

Although there were still two weeks until Christmas, the theme of the cruise was dedicated to the holiday. Or at least to the novelty of the holiday. And because of that, Landon and I had selected an entire wardrobe for our pet that would give us immense pleasure. Luci was rather comfortable walking around naked, and there was always a good time to be had when she was, but I had a penchant for costumes, and this had been an opportunity I couldn't pass up.

As I was skimming through the selection, the door to the room opened and Landon strolled in. His gaze instantly went to Luci, still splayed on the bed.

"Now that's a beautiful sight," he said reverently, walking over to her before glancing my way. "Has she been good?"

"So far, yes."

Landon's smile was wicked as he turned his attention back to her. "Well, that's too bad."

I chuckled, grabbing a sexy red velvet outfit before closing the door.

"There's a meet and greet in an hour," Landon informed me. "In the main ballroom. They'll have appetizers."

"I know." I tossed the outfit on the bed beside her.

"Nice selection," he said, looking at the little red velvet skirt that would do little to cover anything and the equally small bra that would plump her tits but only discretely hide her nipples beneath the white, feathery fringe. "Stockings and heels?"

"Absolutely," I agreed.

Landon peered down at Luci. "Go get dressed, pet. Then you can model for us."

I noticed the pout on Luci's delectable mouth as she said, "Yes, Sir."

When she closed herself into the bathroom, Landon strolled to the balcony and opened the door. I followed him outside. The sun was bright, the breeze warm, bringing with it the scent of the ocean.

"It's packed down there," Landon said, stepping up to the railing.

"I figured it would be. Trent managed to get nearly every Dominant at Dichotomy a room."

"He told me." Landon glanced over at me. "I saw him when I was downstairs. He introduced me to Xander Boone and Mercedes Bryant."

"He works with them," I said, recalling a conversation I'd had with Trent.

"In the past, yes. Xander's in real estate."

I didn't know much about Trent's other business partners. I knew he was a silent partner in a club—Devotion—but he rarely spent much time in Dallas anymore, although he did keep in touch with those people.

"See anyone else?"

"Zeke's here. So are Edge and Cav. Justin was down there. Ian and Isaac. Oh, and I saw Jane."

I had expected all of them. This cruise had been a topic of conversation for the past couple of months, and the Dominants at Dichotomy had shown their intrigue with the idea. If it went well, I could see this becoming a more frequent tradition.

I peered over at my twin. "What about Talon?"

"The rumor is he's coming. As is Ransom."

For whatever reason, I was glad to hear that. It had been a while since I'd talked to Ransom Bishop, and I knew he'd started his new life over on Talon's private island, but I'd still held out hope that one day we would run into him again.

Landon stood tall once more, stared out at the endless water. "We depart in a few minutes. I figure it's a good time to indulge."

I chuckled and turned to head back into the room where Luci was now standing, her hands behind her back, head tilted down.

"Turn around," Landon instructed. "Model for us."

I closed the balcony door and watched as Luci did a slow spin, showing off all that supple, glowing skin. The waist of the little velvet skirt rode low on her hips, and there were only a couple of inches of fabric to cover her pussy and ass. The bra was just as revealing despite the fact her nipples were covered by the white fringe. A light breeze would have it parting, revealing what she was hiding beneath. The white thigh-high stockings were a nice touch, accentuating her legs, and the black, heeled Mary Janes gave her a schoolgirl charm as well as a couple of inches in height.

She looked lovely and I was eager to show her off.

<hr>

LUCI

Turned out, the meet and greet was basically just a regular day at the club.

The enormous ballroom had been decorated for the holidays in blue and silver, but it was the accessories that had captured my attention. Cages, spanking benches, even a St. Andrew's cross had been added and were already being put to good use. Clarissa Tinsley—one of Trent Ramsey's submissives—was draped across the spanking bench while Trent wielded a crop. Case Rhinehart—a masochist who belonged to Zeke—was restrained to the St. Andrew's cross, weights dangling from his balls. And as was usual for these types of settings, there were several other submissives being utilized as furniture and dishes throughout.

I figured I was lucky that I hadn't yet been strung up for all to see or laid out beneath a pile of cold fish. Instead, I was trailing behind Master and Sir, two leashes attached to the leather collar around my neck while they interacted with people they saw on a regular basis as well as a few I hadn't been introduced to yet. I was curious who they were, how Master and Sir knew them, but since it wasn't my place to ask, I kept my mouth shut and my gaze lowered as best I could.

I had vowed to be on my best behavior, at least until I could get a feel for how things were going to play out on this cruise, which wasn't an easy feat for me. I was naturally curious, and I had a dozen questions running through my head on a normal day. Since today was anything but normal, it took effort to keep my lips clamped shut.

"I have reserved us a table for lunch," Sir informed Master. "And I brought something special for our pet."

Something special? That could be a million different things, I figured, and I wasn't sure I was ready for a surprise.

I fought to keep my head down, rather than look at him. I focused on my feet as he led the way across the room, weaving through a handful of large, round tables that were draped in white linen and decked out with place settings.

When we reached what I assumed was our table, Sir dropped his end of one leash and put his hands on my shoulders, guiding me to a chair.

I thought nothing of it until Master pulled it out and held up a hand as he retrieved something from his pocket.

The sound of foil crinkling made the hair on the back of my neck stand on end. There was only one thing that made that sound. A condom.

My jaw unhinged itself as I watched Master roll the condom on what was quite possibly one of the biggest dildos I'd ever seen. The very thick, very lifelike silicone dick wasn't merely secured to the chair but actually part *of* the chair. From the looks of it, the dildo came up from underneath, through a hole in the center. Knowing Master and Sir, it was connected to a fucking machine somehow.

"Sit, pet," Landon instructed. "Slowly."

I didn't need him to clarify that he expected me to take that dildo inside me. I mean, obviously.

I guess I should've been grateful it wasn't a butt plug.

"Yes, Sir," I said easily, gracefully moving so that I could do as instructed.

It took only a moment for me to ease down onto the dildo, my body stretching to accommodate. I couldn't deny that I was wet, my pussy eager for the intrusion. Master and Sir had withheld intercourse for the past week, although they'd made no effort not to claim my mouth whenever they saw fit.

I moaned, a sound that caught the attention of a few others around us.

"All the way down," Master said firmly, holding my arm as I seated myself on the fake dick.

"Good girl," Sir crooned, taking the seat to my left. His was a regular ol' chair, of course. As was Master's.

Both men watched me for a moment and I knew they were assessing my comfort level. While they thoroughly enjoyed tormenting me, I knew they were always worried they might hurt me. Since I did have a safe word and I wasn't using it, they would eventually relax.

As for me … well, relaxing wasn't going to be easy since the dildo was a tad uncomfortable. I could tolerate it for a brief period of time, sure, but I had the increasing desire to fuck myself on it. With every passing second, the urge to do so became nearly impossible to ignore.

"I believe her tension is building," Sir said, his gaze skimming over me slowly.

Master picked up his vodka tonic, took a drink, also watching me. "Is that true, pet?"

"Yes, Master," I said honestly. There was no sense lying to them.

"Would you like some assistance with that?"

"Yes, Master."

Master glanced at Sir, a look passing between them. A second later, Sir retrieved something from his pocket.

I gritted my teeth when he revealed a decorative set of nipple clamps.

And here I'd thought the outfit was going to provide a bit of cover.

"One orgasm will cost you an hour with these on. Is that what you want?"

"Yes, Sir," I blurted, my hips already beginning to gyrate in my efforts to apply some friction.

Without hesitation, Master and Sir pulled the bra cups down enough to reveal my nipples. They hadn't been covered by fabric, only the feather fringe, so it didn't take much. What came next was more brutal than the clamps. Master and Sir both teased my nipples with their fingers, their breath, even their tongue. I was a writhing mess by the time they synchronously placed the clamps on my sensitive nipples.

I cried out as the pleasure/pain zinged from my nipples to my clit. The sound drew the attention of others around us, but I ignored them as best I could. The only thing I cared about right now was coming.

"Please, Master. Sir," I whispered. "May I please fuck myself on the dildo?"

"You may," Sir answered.

Back in the beginning, I would've been horrified by the idea of doing something so intimate with others around. However, the years I'd spent with Master and Sir had desensitized me. I was no longer modest about my needs, no longer worried about being watched.

Placing my hands on the table, I began lifting and lowering myself on the silicone dick, my thighs screaming from the movement even as the pleasure chased the pain away. I couldn't stop myself, my body desperately seeking the relief my Doms had withheld this past week.

"It looks to me like you're already having a good time."

The deep baritone intruded on my efforts but only briefly. I didn't spare Zeke a glance as he turned his attention to Master and Sir while I continued to fuck myself on the cock. The progress I had made faded slightly, but I refused to let them steal this from me.

"I had the cowboy doing something similar earlier," Zeke told Master and Sir. "I do like that you're making her do the work. Perhaps my fuck toys are spoiled."

I did my best to ignore him, but it wasn't easy.

"Do you need some help, pet?" Sir asked, his gaze still locked on me.

"No, Sir." The last time he'd asked me that, I had answered in the affirmative and he had cut me off, refusing to let me come. "But thank you for the offer, Sir."

He chuckled softly, which only renewed my determination.

Shifting my hips, I was able to change the angle of penetration, which was exactly what I needed. My nipples tightened, the clamps sending a bolt of fire through my bloodstream.

"Oh, God," I moaned, tilting my head back and letting the sensation wash over me. "God, yes."

I could practically feel more eyes on me, but in that moment, as the electric current was bearing down on me, I didn't care who watched. The only thing I wanted was—

I screamed as my orgasm ripped through me, stealing the air from my lungs and the starch from my legs.

It was ... fabulous.

SIR
(LANDON)

The majority of the first day of the cruise was spent interacting with people.

Aside from the one orgasm we'd allowed Luci to have earlier in the day, Langston and I had agreed to withhold any more. It was a form of punishment, but not necessarily because she had earned it. More so because I knew if we kept her on edge, she would be able to relax more in this setting.

Luci had certainly come a long way over the years. Back when we had hired her, she'd been an innocent, naive young woman who hadn't yet tapped into her sexual desires. We'd quickly changed that, introducing her to a lifestyle that she had taken to in a way none of us really expected. Initially, we had intended for Luci to be the office fuck toy, someone the four of us could play with when it suited us. She would've been treated like a queen and used like a slut, but not soon after interacting with her, everything changed. My twin and I both had taken to her in a way that shocked everyone, including us. And not long after that, we'd staked our claim.

Now I couldn't imagine our lives without her. She was our everything. Love, light, laughter. She made us whole in a way I'd thought was impossible.

"I instructed her to come out here when she's finished with her shower," Langston said, stepping onto the balcony, two drinks in his hand.

He passed one to me. "Is she tired?"

My brother's smile was wicked. "No. She's … antsy."

I could only imagine. We had done our best to touch her in every way possible throughout the day, but never enough that it would give her any sort of relief.

"Good," I told him, taking a sip of the vodka tonic my twin had taken to making lately.

"I take it you intend to offer some relief."

"I do, yes."

He nodded. "Good. While you do that, I'm going to mingle with some people."

I understood my brother was giving me some alone time with Luci. It was how we did things. Although there were plenty of times we ganged up on her, we also enjoyed those solo moments, too.

"You don't have to. You're welcome to stay. I'm sure she'd enjoy both of us."

Langston smirked. "I'm sure she would. We've got plenty of time for that."

"What's on the agenda for tomorrow?"

"There's a breakfast for us. The submissives will be treated to a few hours of pampering."

"Good. She'll enjoy that."

I knew Luci enjoyed her time with her friends and she had many who were in attendance. Without the Dominants around, they could relax and be themselves.

"I'm sure she will." Langston tossed back the rest of his drink. "Anyway. I'll be back in a bit. Don't wait up."

I chuckled, not bothering to respond. I intended to take my time with Luci, so there was a good chance we would still be up whenever he made his way back.

Half an hour later, Luci walked out onto the balcony wearing nothing but a smile. She had taken the time to dry her long hair, the dark tresses spilling over her shoulders and down her back. She was exquisite in every way.

"Come here." I pointed to the spot in front of me.

Without hesitation, Luci joined me, kneeling on the small pillow I'd brought out for her. She rested her head on my knee, allowed me to slide my hand through her hair.

"You owe me for the orgasm I allowed you to have earlier, don't you, pet?"

"Yes, Sir, I definitely do."

"How do you propose you do that?"

"If it pleases Sir, I could use my mouth."

The little minx. She always got me with that one.

"I like that idea."

When Luci inched back, I pushed my athletic shorts down my hips, freeing my cock before settling back into the chair.

"Start slow," I instructed. "Then you can show me how deep you can take me."

"Yes, Sir." Her eyes glittered with what I'd come to recognize as desire.

Luci was a seductress, even if she didn't realize it. She'd taken our instructions to be graceful to heart, and she put forth the effort in everything she did. Including a blow job. She used her lips and her tongue, carefully caressing my shaft. Up, down. Slowly at first, alternating between sucking and licking, working me up without frenzy.

The attention alone had my cock thickening, but the delicious sensation was enough to relax me. The way she sucked me, careful not to move too fast or too slow. My pet knew exactly how I liked her mouth on my cock.

But a man could only tolerate so much before the need to come became a threat.

I slid my hand over her hair as I watched her lips wrapping around my shaft. "Stop," I instructed when she reached the base. "Take more."

With ease, Luci slid down my cock, her mouth taking the majority of my shaft. The sensitive, swollen head bumped the back of her throat. She gagged, pulled back, then made another attempt. After several tries, I helped her out by applying pressure to the back of her head. I held her in place for longer each time the head of my dick brushed the back of her throat. Before long, she had her nose crushed to my skin, my dick filling her lovely mouth.

I was tempted to come right down her throat but decided to refrain for the moment. I wanted nothing more than to fuck her tight, wet pussy, and coming now wouldn't help my cause.

"Stop," I commanded, gripping her hair and pulling her off my dick.

Luci lifted her head and wiped the saliva from her chin, her eyes still glittering as her gaze met mine.

Before I could instruct her on what to do, I heard a sliding door open, and then voices drifted from our neighbor's balcony.

I instantly recognized them to be the voices of our business partners, Ben Snowden and Justin Parker. Sounded to me like Justin was in full Dom mode, which meant Ben—a Switch— was in submissive mode tonight.

"On your back. Then our sweet girl can sit on your face until I tell you to stop."

I smiled as a shiver ran over Luci. Clearly she enjoyed listening to the action.

Unfortunately for her, I wasn't interested in being a voyeur tonight.

"I think it's time *you* sit on *my* face," I told her as I stood, taking her hand and leading her inside.

After stripping out of my shorts, I dropped onto the king-sized bed and got comfortable before motioning my pet over. She knelt over my face, gripping the headboard and allowing me to enjoy her delectable little pussy. My order for her not to come earned me a grunt, but she managed to refrain despite my efforts to send her careening over the edge.

"Good girl," I said, pulling back enough to look up at her. "Now turn around and ride my cock like you did that toy earlier today."

Her smile was pure sunshine as she quickly maneuvered so that she was riding me reverse cowgirl, my cock buried to the hilt in her slippery wet cunt.

With my hands on her hips, I helped her to rock slowly, not wanting to rush things because I enjoyed making her wait as much as I enjoyed the pleasure that came from the tight clasp of her pussy.

Ten minutes later, Luci was still riding me, only her whimpers had started growing louder by the minute. She didn't ask if she could come because she knew better. If she had, I would've made her wait longer.

I was about to give her permission when the door to our room opened and Langston strolled in. He instantly took in the scene before a smile landed on his face.

"Mind if I join?" he asked, his question obviously for me since Luci didn't have a say in the matter. Granted, I knew what her answer would be if she did.

"I don't mind," I said, thrusting my hips up once before stilling Luci. "You can have her ass." I smacked Luci's hip. "Turn around."

She made quick work of changing positions so she was facing me. This time I pulled her down so I could claim her mouth while Langston undressed and grabbed the lube.

"Fuck me, pet," I whispered as she sank down on my cock. "Fuck me like you love me."

She shivered as she rolled her hips, making love to me in a way I'd never experienced before Luci. She was gentle and sweet, and it was almost enough to send me over that precarious edge.

Her whimpers returned when Langston joined us on the bed. I could feel his finger penetrating her ass as he prepared her for his cock. And finally, Langston's cock joined mine deep inside our pet, him in her asshole, me in her pussy.

"You ready, pet?" Langston's voice was rough.

"Yes, Master."

From that point on, the only thing I could do was ride out the pleasure as Langston unleashed on her, fucking her ass while Luci rode my cock. We drilled her simultaneously, then opposite, again and again, until I could sense she was hanging by a thread.

"You may come now, pet," I growled.

No sooner did the words escape than Luci screamed, her nails digging into my skin as her pussy locked down on my cock. I drove up inside her one final time and let myself go at the same time Langston released in her ass.

A very good first day if I had to say so myself.

Cabin by Candlelight

Logan, Elijah, and Samantha from *Conviction* and *Entrusted*

After eight years of marriage, and seven years into their polyamorous relationship, Logan, Samantha, and Elijah are about to take things to the next level.

Chapter One

Wednesday, December 15, 2021

SAMANTHA MCCOY WOKE UP TO AN EMPTY bed. Not exactly unusual, regardless of whose bed she woke up in. Eight years of marriage and seven years into the polyamorous relationship they had with Elijah Penn and she was still alternating bedrooms much of the time.

Not exactly a problem. Not most of the time, anyway. If she looked at it from a practical standpoint, she had two bedrooms and two bathrooms, both set up with her things as though it was as natural as breathing. So what if she had double the amount of things, at least her pillows were only getting half the use, right?

Oh, sure, they had the playroom where the three of them had fun, something she always looked forward to. But it wasn't the same. It wasn't the same because it wasn't *their* room. It was … it was a sex room, not a bedroom, and by God, Sam wanted *one* room. Just one single room where the three of them could sleep together, dream together. Just *be* together. All the time.

As for what had prompted this crazy idea to combine their lives into one… Well, that was the bigger issue. The one where, on the mornings after a night she spent with Logan, she found herself waking up to an empty bed despite the early hour. The man was working too much and she suspected she knew why. Only he was pretending that it was just business as usual, when in reality, she got the feeling he was working with his twin to come up with a new club design.

If the man only knew he wasn't nearly as subtle as he thought he was. Sam had long ago picked up on his tells, of which he had many. The way he glanced down briefly at the very beginning of an explanation told her he wasn't being entirely truthful. The way he tugged on his left earlobe and glanced to the side told her he was dodging her question entirely. And the way he smoothed his hair back, then rubbed his neck told her he was frustrated with her.

Yep. The man had many tells.

Add that to the fact he spent more time in his home office these days than he ever had before, and Sam was convinced he was up to something. As for why she suspected it was with Luke ... well, that was because Sierra had told her Luke was doing the very same things. The twins were up to something.

"You're awake."

Sam peered over at the door and saw Logan leaning against the jamb. He was dressed in a black Henley and dark jeans, looking as remarkable as the first time she'd seen him. Logan could rock the casual look as easily as he could a suit and tie, but what impressed her more than his smoking-hot body and the washboard abs he hid beneath the designer labels was the sprinkling of gray at his temples. His once black hair was going salt-and-pepper as he aged, and she found it immensely hot.

"Sam?"

"Hmm?"

"Get your mind out of the gutter."

She frowned. "You've never minded that it went there before."

"And I wouldn't now except you've got to finish packing. Our flight leaves in a few hours and we need you to be ready."

"I want a new bed," she blurted, propping herself up and allowing the sheet to slide down below her bare breasts.

Logan's gaze slid from her face to her breasts, just as she'd predicted it would.

"What do you think?" she prompted, discreetly straightening her spine to thrust her chest forward.

He smiled that sexy, mischievous smile that she loved so much.

"About the bed," Sam clarified.

It clearly took effort, but his gaze lifted to her face even as he adjusted himself as though she couldn't see him.

But rather than come at her like a starving man, Logan waltzed over and grabbed the garment bag he used when he was taking his suit on a trip.

"Wait!" she declared, sitting up straight and grabbing the sheet. "Why are you taking a suit with you? This is supposed to be a vacation."

"It is a vacation," he said. "Now get up and get ready."

He turned and slipped out of the room, leaving her fuming behind him.

He was most definitely up to something, but two could play that game.

Sam got out of bed, started toward the bathroom, but made a detour at the last second, heading out of the bedroom. She was naked, but that would only save her time in the long run.

"Good morn—" Elijah's words cut off as he looked up from the iPad in front of him. "Bloody good morning," he muttered, leaning back and watching her as she headed for the coffeepot.

No, Sam would never tire of that. Both of her men were blatant in their desire for her, and that was something she craved like air and water. They had the ability to make her feel like she was the only woman in the world. She had long ago expected the novelty to wear off as she'd heard happened in many relationships, but it hadn't. And for that, Sam felt incredibly blessed.

Pretending she had no ulterior motive for being naked in the kitchen, Sam went to the coffeepot, found her favorite mug already sitting beside it waiting for her. That was Logan's doing, she knew. Elijah's romantic gestures were more overt, and she honestly appreciated them both equally.

She could feel their eyes on her as she poured her coffee, doctored it with cream and sugar, and took a sip to test it.

"Perfect," she said, turning around to face them both as she held the mug with both hands.

She smiled at Eli, loving the way his eyes darkened as he blatantly stared at her nakedness. Something else she appreciated about him was that, even after seven years, he still found her sexy.

"Come here, love," he said with a grin, holding out his arm and gesturing her toward his knee.

Sam waltzed over, casting a sideways look at Logan, who was now standing with his arms crossed over his chest. Obviously he was in a hurry to get out of there, hence the reason she was going to take her time.

Oh, they wouldn't be late, she would make sure of that, too, but if she had to hurry through her shower simply so she could enjoy a little morning greeting from the men she loved, she would certainly rush to make it happen.

But first the morning greeting.

Sam stepped into Eli's arm, let him guide her down to his denim-clad knee as she pretended to only care about the coffee in her hand.

"She thinks she holds all the cards," Eli said.

"She does," Logan agreed, still watching her intently.

"I think she might need a lesson in who's really in charge here." Eli chuckled. "What do you think?"

Sam's gaze swung to Logan as he approached slowly. When he reached down to take her coffee mug, she reluctantly handed it over.

"I think she won't be needing this right now."

LOGAN WAS FAIRLY CERTAIN HIS WIFE WAS going to be the death of him.

Not that he was complaining about the fact she was tormenting him with her naked form, wandering through the house without a stitch on as though it was an everyday occurrence. Sure, if he had his way, she would be naked a majority of the time. Her long, dark blond hair hanging down her back and over her shoulder, her light green eyes glittering with mischief and promise. Those sultry lips, her luscious tits, the gentle curve of her waist, the sexy swell of her hips, and the sweet juncture between her trim thighs. Every inch of her beckoned to every inch of him, even when he knew they didn't have time to waste.

After setting her coffee mug on the counter, Logan returned to where she was perched on Eli's thigh. Sam smiled up at him, clearly daring him to do his worst, and he suspected she thought he wouldn't.

But Logan wasn't the sort of man who backed down from a dare, and he damn sure wasn't about to start now.

"I haven't had breakfast yet," he said, holding her gaze. "And now I know what I'm hungry for."

He loved the way Sam's eyes glazed over at the promise in his tone.

Logan held out his hand to her, waited to see if she would take it. She glanced at Eli and smiled before laying her hand in his, allowing Logan to help her to her feet. It had been a while since they'd enjoyed an early-morning feast at this table, and today seemed like as good a day as any.

"What are you doing?" Sam asked with a giggle when Logan spun her around and backed her against it.

"Breakfast is the most important meal of the day, is it not?"

Her eyes remained locked on his face as he assisted her onto the table, urging her back until he could settle her heels on the edge. He wasn't rough, but he wasn't gentle, positioning her the way he wanted her, loving the way her nipples pebbled into hard little points.

"You do know if we miss our flight, I will paddle your ass," he grumbled, pressing her knees wide.

"Then you should let me take a shower," she countered.

"Too late for that."

Logan leaned in and breathed in the musky scent of her sex as he used his fingers to separate her slick folds, admiring her lovely pussy. He let his breath fan over her flesh, enjoying the way her stomach tightened and her legs trembled with anticipation. His wife did love having her pussy eaten, and since it was one of his favorite things, too, these encounters were a frequent occurrence in this house.

When Elijah reached over to cup her breast, thumbing her nipple until it drew up impossibly tight, Logan leaned in and swept his tongue over her. He lightly licked her entrance then her clit, but he wasn't about to give her what she wanted. He sucked on her labia, realizing she'd been waxed smooth very recently, something he found immensely erotic.

"Logan..."

He ignored her plea, taking his time, licking and laving her delicate flesh, alternating to ensure he didn't stimulate one spot too much. He was not about to make her come yet. That would take all the fun out of it.

Sam grunted, clearly catching on to his plan. She attempted to thrust her hips to get him where she wanted him, but he played her easily, moving with her and chuckling before finally stepping back.

"Damn you," she hissed, glaring up at him.

Logan smirked as he moved around to the other side of the table. "Eli, why don't you do the honors of finishing her off."

Sam wiggled as Eli got to his feet.

"My pleasure."

Logan curled his hand under Sam's chin, tilted her head back as he leaned down and pressed an upside-down kiss to her mouth.

"If you're really good, I might let you come."

"You wouldn't dare," she whispered on a moan when Eli's face pressed between her thighs.

Logan couldn't fight the desire to watch the man as he feasted on Sam's pussy. This was one of the highlights of his day, watching the two of them together. He couldn't explain why he was so fascinated with watching another man pleasure his wife, but it was there all the same. Had been since the beginning, but if he was being honest, it hadn't been until Eli came into the picture that his world had felt complete.

Sam's back bowed, her knees falling wide as Eli's tongue glided through her slit. He teased her clit momentarily, flicking the little bundle of nerves until Sam was writhing on the table.

"How does it feel, baby?" Logan prompted.

"Good. So good."

When she reached for Eli's head to hold him in place, Logan stopped her, taking both of her arms and positioning them over her head. He kept a firm hand on her so she was at Eli's mercy while the man drove her wild.

If they hadn't been pressed for time, Logan would've pulled his aching dick out and let his wife work him with her delectable mouth. But that would definitely stall them longer than was necessary. There would be time for that later, when they were in their Colorado cabin. One week in the mountains was just what the doctor ordered. At least he hoped. Provided Sam and Eli didn't get angry when they realized he had business to tend to while he was there. It wouldn't take much time, but it would take him away from them for a short while. He figured they would have plenty to keep them occupied while he was away though.

"Eli ... oh, God ... please ... I need..."

"Tell him, Sam," Logan ordered. "Tell him what you want."

"Make me come," she pleaded.

Logan's eyes never left Eli as he continued to suckle her clit while dipping one finger into her pussy. It was a sensual scene, one Logan would never tire of. Even these too-brief moments were worth it.

"I should make you wait," Eli mumbled against her smooth flesh. "I should make you wait for taunting us with this sweet pussy."

Sam's head tilted back when Eli thrust two fingers inside her. "No. Please. Don't make me wait."

"It would serve you right," Logan taunted.

"Eli ... oh, God ... please!"

Logan peered down at Sam's face, met her gaze when she opened her eyes. He held her stare and smirked. "Make her come, Eli."

Her eyes widened and he could see the pleasure darken the light green of her irises. Her body shuddered, her fingers clutching his wrists as he held her arms in place.

"You ready, baby?"

Sam nodded, moaning louder now.

Logan didn't look away from her face as Eli sent her spiraling right over the crest and into ecstasy, Eli's name spilling from Sam's lips.

God, she was something else.

Chapter Two

IF ELIJAH COULD'VE AVOIDED AIRPORTS, HE WOULD'VE done so. It wasn't so much the flying that frustrated him as much as the hassle and the time it took to get from one place to another. Two hours early, waiting, boarding, flying, getting luggage. He could think of a million things he would rather be doing. When it was work-related, he tended to pass the time easily, always connected to his email, his files. But this wasn't work and he had long ago decided he would disconnect whenever he could. And since he enjoyed spending time with Logan and Sam far more than work, it wasn't a hardship.

The past few hours had stressed him more than he anticipated, and now that they'd made it to their destination, he was focused on breathing, relaxing, letting all that tension drain away. Now that they were finally at the cabin, he couldn't find much to complain about. Despite the concerning weather situation that they'd learned about upon their arrival, this was the perfect getaway. Quiet, secluded. Homey.

The cabin was a two-story log structure with vaulted ceilings in the living room, three bedrooms upstairs, a game room, media room, a fully stocked kitchen, and half a dozen fireplaces that could be used for warmth. It looked as though it would sleep a dozen comfortably, which meant the three of them would have it made for the next seven days.

And then there was the outdoors.

The snow was banked near the windows, but it was a sight to behold. Especially since he couldn't remember the last time he'd seen a snowfall, save for the ice storm they'd endured at the first part of this year. But he figured that didn't really count. It hadn't looked like this for more than five minutes.

Logan certainly knew how to plan a vacation, even if Elijah knew Logan wasn't here solely for vacation. The man had an ulterior motive, which was par for the course for the McCoy brothers. Elijah had long ago gotten used to the way that Logan and Luke managed to finagle time for work regardless of the event. If Elijah was right, this particular vacation was going to be expensed out. At least partially, anyway.

"What're you thinking about?"

Elijah glanced over his shoulder to see Sam approaching. She looked downright edible in her oversized black sweater, patterned leggings, and her favorite Ugg boots. She'd clearly come with the intention of getting cozy and Elijah was grateful for that. He was looking forward to some downtime with her.

She stepped up behind him, pressed a kiss to his shoulder and then stared out the window beside him.

"It's beautiful," she said, her voice reflecting the same awe he felt.

Elijah put his arm around her shoulder and pulled her into his side. He pressed a kiss to the top of her head. "It certainly is."

"We needed this, you know?"

He did know. There never seemed to be enough time in the day to really slow down. Between work and their busy social calendar, there wasn't a lot of relaxation. In the beginning, Elijah had kept himself somewhat separated from Sam and Logan's extended family, but over time his attempts became futile. The McCoy clan had welcomed him with open arms, making him feel as though he'd always been meant to be with them. And then there was Devotion, the club where they spent a good majority of their time, mingling with friends, indulging in one another.

The thought made him smile.

He had to admit, he'd never been happier in his life. And that was saying something considering, at one point, he'd thought happiness was not something he would be blessed with again. Not the case. Sam had made sure of it.

"So what's on the agenda?" Sam asked, turning so that she was in front of him.

"I can think of a few things."

"I just heard the weather's supposed to be getting bad," Logan said as he strolled into the room, his phone in his hand, eyes glued to the screen. "Really bad."

"If we're lucky, we won't lose power," Sam told him, her gaze still fixed on the outdoors. "And I know we can think of a dozen ways to keep ourselves occupied indoors."

Elijah looked at Logan's reflection in the glass, knew he was thinking about whatever meeting he was supposed to attend while he was here. He hadn't said as much, but Elijah had learned to read Logan as easily as he could read Sam.

After pressing one more kiss to Sam's head, Elijah released her and turned from the window. "Who're you supposed to meet while we're here?"

Logan's eyes flew to his face and he frowned.

"There's no sense denying it," Sam added. "We're not dumb. We know you've got business while you're here. It's what you do."

Logan sighed. "It's not until Friday afternoon."

"Then I suggest we make the most of the days before then," Elijah told him, "and worry about Friday when it gets here."

"I like the way you think. How about lunch?"

Elijah peered down at Sam, smiled. "Are you offering to cook?"

She teasingly smacked his arm. "I'm a great cook."

"I wouldn't go so far as to say *great*," Logan joked, losing that frustrated look.

Sam stood taller, back straight. "That's not what you said when I made chicken piccata," she countered.

"If I recall, you gave me a blow job shortly after dinner," Logan noted, moving toward her.

Elijah chuckled. She had given him a blow job while Elijah had volunteered for dish duty. He certainly hadn't minded watching the show while he worked.

"What does that have to do with anything?" Sam's forehead creased as though she'd just understood. "Wait. Are you saying you praised my cooking so I would suck your dick?"

Logan laughed, a booming sound that was contagious, making Elijah laugh, too.

"Y'all suck," Sam pouted, stomping toward the kitchen.

Before she could get too far, Logan grabbed her around the waist and hoisted her up off the ground. "I'm kidding. Your cooking is … divine?"

Sam elbowed him and Elijah laughed at them both. This was part of the appeal of their relationship. The fact that they enjoyed one another's company enough that they could joke about something as mundane as cooking made it so easy to be with them.

"Why don't I cook?" Elijah volunteered. "Then we'll take turns from here on out."

Logan put Sam back on her feet and they both grinned wide.

It was Elijah's turn to frown. "Wait. You two did this on purpose."

Sam giggled and strolled his way, throwing her arms around his neck. "Your cooking is *so* much better than mine."

"You manipulated me?"

She planted a kiss on his cheek. "Never."

"You little minx," he mumbled, holding her against him. "You'll pay for that later."

Sam's voice was but a whisper in his ear when she said, "I'm looking forward to it."

THEIR LATE LUNCH/EARLY DINNER CONSISTED OF soup and sandwiches, something Sam could've easily prepared if they hadn't given her crap about her cooking skills. Not that she was denying she wasn't as brilliant in the kitchen as Elijah, but she could hold her own. Especially with tomato soup and grilled cheese.

However, she hadn't pitched a fit, enjoying the meal in the dining area while the three of them admired the view out the floor-to-ceiling windows that overlooked the mountain they were perched upon. This was the very reason she had agreed to come. The view was breathtaking and certainly not something she could see back home. Big, fluffy snowflakes floated down from the sky, layering the ground in white. It was serene and she looked forward to cozying up with hot cocoa, a warm fire, and a good book at some point.

After lunch, Sam had left both men to take care of the dishes while she went to unpack her things.

Because there were enough rooms for everyone, Sam had commandeered one of her own, selecting one with a large vanity in the bathroom where she could put her stuff. She wouldn't sleep in a room by herself, but it would give her a space all her own where she could take naps, read, or just daydream. This was vacation, after all, and she fully intended to leave here relaxed and in good spirits.

No sooner did that thought flutter through her brain than the power blinked.

Frowning, Sam wandered out of the room to the second-floor landing that overlooked the main living area. From there she could see out the enormous windows that ran the length of the back of the cabin. Beyond, she could see thick, dark clouds looming overhead. Definitely a storm coming.

On the main floor, she heard Logan and Elijah talking, their voices hushed, something they did from time to time when they pulled that alpha male stunt of trying to protect the little lady.

"What's going on?" she insisted, her voice carrying as she started down the stairs. "Why are y'all whispering?"

"We're not whispering, love," Elijah answered, his tone placating.

Sam glared at him when she reached the first floor. "Don't do that, Eli. Tell me what's going on."

"It's just the storm," Logan assured her, his eyes on his phone. "This is the front side of it."

Sam glanced out the windows again, and for the first time since they'd arrived, she thought about what it would mean if they lost electricity while they were here.

"Is there a backup generator?" she wondered aloud.

"No," Elijah answered easily. "But we've got enough firewood to last us through the winter if we needed to."

She spun around to face him. "That's not funny."

Sam still remembered what it was like back in February when the ice storm hit Texas. They'd been without power for nearly a week, and almost as long without water. It had been horrible, especially since they hadn't been prepared for that sort of storm. No one had because Texas wasn't prone to snow, only the occasional light dusting, but mostly they were iced over from rain when the temperatures would get low enough. Again, a rarity for them.

"Come here," Elijah urged, taking her hand and leading her over to the leather sectional sofa that faced the enormous rock-faced fireplace. "I'll start a fire just in case."

Sam plopped down on the sofa and watched as Elijah went to work. Admittedly, it was easy to forget her worries when she was watching him. The way he moved, the way he spoke ... there was something enigmatic about Elijah Penn, something that called to her on a base level.

Like Logan, Elijah was a couple of years shy of fifty but didn't look a day over forty. His dark hair was thick and didn't have a single touch of silver. His brown eyes had softened over the years, losing some of the pain and storm clouds she'd noticed when they first met. And his body ... she couldn't think about his very fine, very toned form without getting hit with a bolt of lust.

Warm hands settled on her shoulders and Sam glanced back to see Logan.

"This should pass easily tonight," he said, as though that would assure her. "There's another storm predicted for tomorrow, but it should move through quickly."

"So you're our very own meteorologist?" She tried to keep her tone light, but it wasn't easy. Considering Logan had used this vacation as an excuse for work—or quite possibly he'd used work as an excuse for this vacation—Sam was irked.

However, the good news was, he would be all in for a couple of days since his meeting wasn't until Friday afternoon. Likely, that was the only reason Logan was paying attention to the weather at all. Otherwise, they would've been enjoying themselves, right?

Speaking of...

Sam shook off the worry and fear of the weather. It would do no good for them to sit here and fret over something they couldn't control. The last thing she wanted was to spend her vacation getting herself all worked up and in worse shape than when she'd left Dallas.

She took a deep breath and relaxed back against the cushion, allowing Logan to massage the tenseness from her shoulders.

Once the fire was burning, the warmth from the flames was immediate, relaxing her even more.

"What shall we do to pass the time?" Elijah asked when he came to sit on the sofa, patting the cushion, his request for Sam to put her feet in his lap.

Giddy over the idea of a foot massage, Sam twisted so he could have her feet. He easily slipped her boots from her feet, dropping them to the floor before peeling off her socks. Sam flexed her toes and smiled at him.

Logan joined them, taking his position so she could rest her head in his lap.

Ah, now this was what she'd been looking forward to.

"We could play a game," Logan suggested.

"Truth or dare," Sam blurted, glancing down at Elijah.

She watched him roll his eyes.

Sam chuckled. "What? You know you like that game."

"We *always* play that game," Logan said, likely speaking what Elijah was thinking.

She canted her head back to look up at him. "You said you liked it."

"That was until the last time," Elijah answered.

"When you chose *truth* every time," Logan finished.

Sam frowned. "I did not."

"Oh, yes, you did."

"I won't pick truth."

"Then that's not really truth or dare, now is it?" Logan commented.

Sam blew out a frustrated breath. "Fine. What would you prefer we did?"

It didn't surprise her when Logan reached for the remote.

Well, at least she was getting a foot rub out of this deal.

Chapter Three

Friday, December 17, 2021

LOGAN WOKE UP EARLY ON FRIDAY MORNING, feeling relaxed from a full day of doing nothing. They'd spent the rest of Wednesday and all day Thursday lounging around, watching movies, eating popcorn, and chilling. The weather hadn't gotten as bad as they'd thought it would, and aside from a couple of blinks, they hadn't lost power, which had kept Sam in a good mood.

It had been nice just to relax and enjoy some time off.

Enough so, Logan had stopped fretting over the business meeting that was scheduled for later today. That was, until last night when he'd gone to bed alone since it was Elijah's night with Sam. Without her there to keep him company, he'd had no choice but to let his mind wander, and whenever that happened, it tended to gravitate toward work.

After an hour of tossing and turning, unable to go back to sleep, Logan decided it was time to get up. He could have some coffee and spend a couple of hours going over the proposal that Luke expected him to give to a new set of investors.

He pulled on a pair of pajama pants and a long-sleeve T-shirt, then headed downstairs.

"I didn't think you'd be up this early."

Lost in his own thoughts, Logan jolted, his gaze slamming into Elijah, who was sitting at the small dining room table with a cup of coffee in his hand.

"I didn't think *you'd* be up this early," Logan countered.

Elijah smiled. "I'm still on Dallas time."

Logan understood that. If they went by the clock, they should've still been asleep thanks to the one-hour time difference.

"Coffee's fresh," Elijah said, nodding toward the kitchen.

"Thanks." Logan caught a glimpse of Elijah's iPad screen. "What're you looking at?"

Elijah sighed, setting the tablet down and picking up his mug. "I think Sam's angling to have us in one room."

Logan poured his coffee, his eyes sliding over to Elijah. "She mentioned it to you, too?"

"In her roundabout way, yes." Elijah laughed.

That was Sam for you. When she wanted something, she rarely came out and asked. Instead, she manipulated and seduced until she got what she wanted. It was one of the things Logan adored about her. There was nothing simple about his wife.

Logan carried his coffee mug to the table, eased into a chair. "What're your thoughts on that?"

Elijah's dark eyes met his, holding steady. "I'll give her anything she wants, Logan. You know that."

"Even if it means sharing a bed with me every night?"

They'd never actually talked about what would happen if and when their relationship ever progressed to this point. They had separate bedrooms and they shared Sam equally for the most part, although Logan was fairly certain Elijah gave up time with her because he didn't want to take from Logan. In the beginning, they'd given Elijah a wide berth because he had preferred more time alone. However, the past few years had changed him, and Logan had noticed that Elijah and Sam had grown rather close.

Elijah smirked. "I love her enough to deal with your snoring, too."

Logan laughed.

It was true, their relationship was unconventional. They both loved Sam, and they both lusted for her. Logan had a penchant for watching Sam be pleasured by Elijah and he wouldn't apologize for it. There was nothing between him and Elijah, though. Well, nothing beyond the natural progression of a relationship such as theirs. They were close. They talked about work and personal things, did things together. All in all, Logan enjoyed Elijah's company immensely.

As far as an attraction to Elijah went, Logan wasn't sure he could explain what it was he felt. Not because he didn't want to, but more so because he didn't understand it himself. Over the years he'd found he was attracted to Elijah, but he didn't think it was a sexual attraction. Simply put, Logan was comfortable around Elijah, more so than he'd ever imagined he would be. But regardless of what he did or didn't feel, he would never take that for granted.

Logan nodded toward the iPad. "So you were looking for a bed?"

"I figured if it would work, we'd need something bigger than a king."

They would. Logan's twin brother had a bed that'd been made for three, which offered more room than a standard king-size did. Considering Logan was six five, the more space, the better.

"Are you thinking a Christmas present?" Logan asked.

Elijah met his gaze again. "If you think it's a good idea, it's definitely worth considering."

Logan peered up at the second floor. "Perhaps we should try sleeping in the same bed while we're here."

"Trial run?" Elijah nodded. "I think that can be arranged."

Logan glanced at the clock on the microwave. "Since it's still early, maybe we head back that way now. Grab a couple more hours, then wake her up appropriately."

Elijah's grin widened. "I like the way you think, McCoy."

SAM WOKE FEELING AS THOUGH SHE'D BEEN sleeping on the surface of the sun.

The heat was everywhere. At her front, her back.

It took a moment to orient herself, remembering they were in Colorado at the cabin Logan had rented for their winter vacation. She peeked open her eyes, saw her husband's handsome face. His eyes were closed and he was breathing heavily, signifying he was still asleep.

Figuring she would get up and grab coffee, Sam rolled to her back but she didn't get far. In fact, she didn't get anywhere thanks to the warm body pressed up against her on the other side.

She stilled instantly and realized that something was seriously off.

For starters, she'd gone to bed with Elijah, which made having Logan in bed with her the first strange thing.

Secondly, she'd gone to bed with Elijah, which meant having them both in the same bed with her—while sleeping— was another strange thing.

Despite the fact they did a lot of interesting activities together in a bed, they never fell asleep in the same room. Even when they were enjoying playtime at home and Sam would drift off, she knew one of them would always move her to their bed before they let themselves succumb to sleep. It was just how it worked.

So this ... *this* was weird.

"What's going on?" she mumbled, staring up at the ceiling as she shifted so she could lie on her back between them.

"Morning, love," Elijah whispered, his warm lips brushing her shoulder.

"Why are the three of us in bed together?"

"We thought that was what you wanted."

Sam frowned, looked over at Elijah, but she couldn't say anything.

Yes, it was what she wanted. More than anything, in fact. However, she hadn't mentioned it to either of them. Not outright anyway. Not yet.

"We've got your number, love," Elijah said, his words spoken softly near her ear. "We know what you're angling for."

"No, you don't."

"One bed. The three of us."

Sam narrowed her gaze, staring at him. Before she could give her own reasons, Elijah shifted closer. Close enough he put his heavy thigh over her leg, pinning her in place while he kissed his way up her neck while at the same time sliding the sheet down to bare her breasts.

"Mmm. This is a great way to wake up in the morning," Logan mumbled.

Sam's head snapped over, her eyes landing on his face. Logan hadn't moved, but his eyes were open, and he was watching as Elijah's oral ministrations worked their way to her breasts.

Her entire body flashed with heat as it always did when Logan watched. There was something innately erotic about her husband watching her with Elijah. She knew he loved it, and partly because of that, she did, too.

Elijah's finger tapped her chin before urging her to turn her head as he moved over her. She accepted the weight of him, spreading her legs to welcome him closer.

"You're so soft," Elijah muttered, his lips trailing over her chin. "So warm and wet."

Sam moaned.

"You ready for me?"

"God, yes."

It was the truth, although she sometimes didn't understand how easily her body prepared for her men. They could make her wet with just a look, and while she enjoyed foreplay, it wasn't always necessary.

Sam wrapped her legs around Elijah's waist and shifted her pelvis to welcome him into her body.

His thick cock stretched her perfectly, filling her slowly as he eased his way in. He grazed every sensitive nerve ending, lighting her up from the inside out.

The sheet slid lower, cool air wafting over her leg.

"Let me watch," Logan whispered, his face moving closer to hers.

Sam knew what he wanted, so she lowered her legs to the bed, while Elijah pushed himself up with his arms, his hips rocking as he pushed in deep, retreated slowly. With the angle of his body, Sam could easily watch as he sank into her, which was what Logan was obviously fascinated by.

"Feels good," she moaned, relaxing as he did all the work to pleasure her.

"I love watching his cock slide into your cunt, your juices coating him," Logan said, his voice a rough, gravelly rasp.

Her skin tingled, her nipples pebbling tighter as his words caressed her in much the same way Elijah was.

This was what she longed for. The three of them together. Logan finding pleasure in watching them together, Sam seeking the comfort both men could give her, and Elijah letting her love him.

Elijah's dark hair fell over his forehead, and Sam brushed it back, staring up at him, accepting that he was going to torment her slowly this morning. She clenched her inner muscles when he pushed in deep, eliciting a ragged groan as his eyes met hers.

"Do that again," he ordered roughly.

Sam did it again and again, clasping him tightly each time he bottomed out inside her.

Before long, Elijah's slow and gentle ride turned frantic. He began pumping his hips, rocking into her harder, deeper, faster.

Logan's hand slid down over her belly, his fingers joining in the party, ruthlessly rubbing her clit as she raced toward that inevitable peak.

"Eli … Logan…" Sam let herself go, falling into the heavenly abyss as her orgasm crested.

Elijah growled low in his throat as he pushed up to his knees, gripping her legs. He didn't stop fucking her, his eyes locked on her face. Sam watched him, loving how sexy he was when he was chasing his release.

"Come for us," Logan commanded.

Elijah's gaze shot to Logan's face, and for the first time in their history together, he came while looking at Logan rather than at her.

And something about that moment triggered an eruption in her that had her crying out once more.

"My turn," Logan rumbled, wasting no time as he took Elijah's place between her legs.

Sam cried out when he filled her, slamming in hard and deep. Elijah moved to her side, his face close to hers, right there in the moment with them.

"Touch her," Logan bit out.

Elijah's hand cupped her breast, his forefinger and thumb pinching her nipple, sending heat bolting straight to her clit.

Logan leaned forward, his body hovering over hers but ensuring he didn't get in Elijah's way.

"Fuck, yes," he growled low in his throat, hammering away at her.

Sam's entire body was tightening again, another cataclysmic eruption looming. She loved this. Loved when they ganged up on her. It was such a rarity that she'd long ago stopped wishing for these moments.

Elijah's hand followed the same route Logan's had earlier, slipping between their bodies until he was strumming her clit, making her body vibrate with the impending release.

Sam gripped Logan's bicep with one hand, the other sliding into Elijah's hair as she held on, her body rocking beneath the onslaught of Logan's powerful thrusts.

Logan groaned, his head tipping back, and Sam peered down her body to where Elijah's hand was. Not only was he thumbing her clit, his knuckles were rubbing against Logan, gliding over his cock every time he retreated. Seeing Elijah touching Logan was more than she could bear. She screamed out their names as her orgasm obliterated her.

Logan followed her right over the edge, slamming into her one final time, pinning Elijah's hand between their bodies as he came with a roar.

WHILE SAM AND LOGAN FOUGHT TO CATCH their breath, Elijah remained where he was. He kept his hand on Sam's stomach as Logan slid to her other side. He was hesitant to look at the man, not sure what he was going to find. Touching Logan had been a serious risk, something he had never intended. He'd been so caught up in that moment, so turned on by watching Logan fucking Sam, he hadn't given it much thought.

Never before had he been inclined to touch a man, but he would admit—at least to himself—that it had been building for a while now. Years, maybe. But only where Logan was concerned.

He blamed his curiosity on the easy relationship they shared. They were bonded by their love for Sam, brought closer by their desire to take care of her, to love her, to pleasure her. And though Elijah had never been attracted to a man before, he found a curiosity about Logan that he couldn't seem to shake. It had grown more intense these past couple of years, and until today, he'd been able to ignore it.

"That was…" Sam exhaled. "That was so hot."

Elijah refused to look at her or Logan, instead staring down at his hand where it rested on her belly.

"I'd have to agree," Logan said, his voice rougher than usual.

Elijah's gaze darted over. Logan was lying on his back, his arm draped over his eyes.

"Which part?" Elijah asked, keeping his tone light.

"For one, waking up to both of you in my bed," she said.

Yeah, Elijah would agree. He did enjoy the idea of waking up every day to Sam, not just on his dedicated days.

"Then the taking turns thing…" Sam giggled. "A girl can get used to that."

Elijah choked on a laugh. "You sound spoiled."

"Oh, I am. Most definitely."

Figuring that was where the conversation would end, Elijah leaned in to kiss her shoulder, preparing to get out of bed and head for the shower, but Sam stopped him with a hand on his arm.

"The hottest part, though?"

He pretended to adjust the sheet to avoid eye contact.

"Was when you fucking touched me," Logan growled. "Holy fuck."

Elijah stilled.

"God, yes," Sam agreed. "I don't think I've ever come so hard before."

"Me, either," Logan chimed in.

Because he had no desire to get into an in-depth conversation about what prompted him to do it, Elijah forced a laugh and rolled out of bed. He padded toward the bathroom since this was the room he'd chosen for himself. He relieved himself then got into the shower.

He was grateful no one intruded on his moment because he needed a minute to get his bearings.

Chapter Four

WHEN ELIJAH DISAPPEARED INTO THE BATHROOM, SAM turned to Logan. She watched him as he lowered his arm and opened one eye to peer over at her, evidently sensing she was staring at him.

"Yes?" he drawled.

"That was insanely hot, right?" she whispered, unable to contain her excitement.

"It was."

She watched him, wondering if he would elaborate. Of course, he didn't.

"Wow," she said, falling back again. "Not sure what'll top that."

"Sam." His tone was etched with warning.

"What?"

"Don't push this."

She turned her head his way. "Push what?"

"Let it be. If it plays out, it plays out."

"Are you saying...?" Sam wasn't even sure what question she wanted to ask. Was her husband actually saying he was interested in something more from Elijah? Perhaps a little man-on-man action?

"I'm saying let it be."

"But—"

"I'm not discussing this with you right now," he grumbled. "Let it go for now."

She found herself left with no choice when Logan got up from the bed and padded out of the room. Her gaze bounced between the bedroom door and the bathroom door while her brain continued to process what had transpired.

Never in the seven years that the three of them had been together had Elijah or Logan touched one another so ... so intimately. Sure, there was touching involved, but it was the natural kind. One man moved against another when changing positions and whatnot. But that wasn't what had happened. Elijah had deliberately stroked Logan's cock with his knuckles while Logan had been fucking her.

Just the thought had a shiver racing through her and a torrent of dirty, filthy fantasies racing through her brain.

Of course, Logan's words were now echoing in her head, too.

Let it be. If it plays out, it plays out.

Let it be? Was he serious? Did he not know her at all?

By the time midafternoon rolled around, Sam was beginning to feel a bit antsy. Part of that was due to the fact they hadn't been able to get out of the cabin due to the weather. Instead, they'd passed the time relaxing. She had curled up with a book, taken a nap, vegged on chips, then taken another nap. All in all, she had managed to while away three whole hours. When Logan had woken her to see if she wanted a late lunch, she had opted for a shower while they cooked.

And now that the meal had been consumed, the dishes washed and put away, Sam was hoping they didn't intend to watch television for the rest of the afternoon. Especially not when they could be doing something together. For instance, playing a game.

"What time's your meeting?" Elijah asked.

Sam's gaze darted to Logan. How had she forgotten he was going to work? It had slipped her mind completely.

"They've rescheduled for Monday," he said, his frustration evident.

If they had rescheduled, then that meant Logan was the one seeking something from them. Otherwise, Logan would've been in control of the time and location, and he was a stickler for punctuality. No doubt her husband would've tackled a blizzard head on just to be on time.

"Did they say why?" she asked, wondering if he might share some details.

"The weather. They said it's predicted to get worse before it gets better."

"Enough that they're willing to postpone a meeting?" Sam didn't understand. "Aren't they used to snow here?"

"They are, but they know I'm not. It's my understanding I might get stranded one way or another if I attempt to head to Denver."

Well, that would suck. Sam didn't like the idea of Logan stranded anywhere. Certainly not away from her and Elijah.

"It'll wait until Monday," he said, his tone soothing. "I do need to call Luke, though. Give him a heads-up."

Sam watched Logan head up the stairs. The cell reception in the cabin was spotty at best, but they'd found it was best on the second floor.

"You okay?" Elijah asked as he walked past her on his way to the living room.

Sam nodded, then turned toward the windows. Only then did she realize it was rather dark outside. Since it was still relatively early—a little after three—she had expected there to be more light. A quick glance at the sky and she saw the reason. Thick, dark clouds loomed overhead, seemingly closer to earth than usual. She figured that had something to do with the altitude. Or maybe it was just a figment of her imagination.

"What do you want to do?" Elijah's voice echoed in the open space. "Movie?"

Sam put the weather out of her mind. There was nothing she could do about it, and since it had gotten Logan to stay here, she figured it might be a blessing.

"I think I'm TV'd out," she admitted, heading for the kitchen just as Logan made it to the bottom of the stairs.

What she wanted to do was play a game, but she wasn't sure how to broach the subject. She'd been shot down quickly the first night they were here, but now she had more motivation to get them to participate. *And* she had a new game she wanted to play, one that she'd found online and purchased for exactly a scenario such as this one.

"She's plotting."

Elijah's voice yanked Sam out of her thoughts, had her gaze darting over to where he was sitting on the sofa.

"She's always plotting," Logan agreed, grabbing two beers from the fridge then delivering one to Elijah on his way to sit down.

"I am not."

"Remember when we used to paddle her ass for lying?" Logan asked, grinning around the lip of his beer bottle. "I think we need to start doing that again."

Sam poured a glass of wine and joined them, but rather than sitting on the couch, she took a seat on the thick, plush rug laid out on the floor, her back to the fireplace.

Logan immediately reached for the remote and Sam gritted her teeth.

"There's a hockey game on," he said, as though reading her shift in mood.

There was always a hockey game on. And when it wasn't hockey, it was baseball or basketball or football. She didn't know when it had happened, but at some point, her husband had developed a penchant for sports.

Almost as though a higher power was siding with her, the power chose that exact moment to flash off. Only this time, it didn't blink back on immediately.

Sam sat motionless as the darkness settled over them. The firelight and the dim light from outside were enough to see by, but the shadows grew heavier throughout the space.

She hated the dark. Like this, anyway. Especially in a place she wasn't completely familiar with. Add in the cold and the snow and—

"Looks like that storm's here," Logan said, sounding relaxed and not at all fazed about the lack of electricity.

"Good thing they postponed," Elijah chimed in.

Sam stared at them, feeling a mixture of anxiety and panic churning inside her. She did not want to spend days without electricity again. That had been brutal the last time. Sure, they had the firewood so they wouldn't get too cold, but that would only go so far.

"Sam, it's all right."

Her gaze shot to Logan's.

"The power'll be back soon, I'm sure."

He had no way of knowing that, but she didn't care to argue with him. It wasn't going to help the situation.

"What if we played a game," Elijah suggested.

She looked at him. "Seriously?"

"Anything but truth or dare," Logan added.

"I've got one," she admitted, letting her focus shift from the darkness to the small silk bag in her pocket. "And no, it's not truth or dare."

Logan's gaze was pinned on her hand. "What do you have?"

"It's called Naughty but Dice," she said with a grin. "I bought it online."

"Dice?" Elijah shifted, his eyes on her.

"Yes." She opened the bag and poured the dice onto the floor in front of her.

With her body blocking the firelight, there was too much of a shadow to see, so she moved to the side.

"This is a sex game."

It wasn't a question, but she responded to Logan anyway. "It's … yes, it's a sex game. You roll the dice and do what it instructs you to do."

"What exactly is on these dice?" Logan asked.

"One has the action, such as kiss or lick or suck," she said, turning the die to read the various sides. "The other has the location, such as neck, ears, lips…"

"So it's tame?"

"Well…" Sam smiled shyly. "There is a triple x side of the die, so you could have to, you know, suck something."

"Who does what?" Elijah asked.

"The person who rolls the dice gets it done to them," she explained.

Sam noticed that Logan looked at Elijah, but Elijah seemed to be avoiding looking at Logan.

"When you roll the dice, who does it to you?" Logan asked.

"That's where I want to improvise."

"Bloody hell," Elijah mumbled.

Sam smiled. "I want to spin the bottle to see who has to … perform."

"Samantha," Logan rumbled in warning.

Ignoring him, she continued to clarify. "The person whose turn it is will spin the bottle. Whoever the bottle lands on or is closest to is the performer. Then the person with the dice will roll them. The performer will then do whatever the dice instructs them to do for one minute, no longer than two."

Her gaze shifted to Elijah and she saw that he was watching her closely. She couldn't read his expression, but she could tell he was uncomfortable, and she instantly felt like an ass.

"I'm sorry," she blurted, setting her wineglass on the nearby end table. "We don't have to play."

Elijah's eyebrows lowered but he didn't speak.

And now she felt like complete crap for putting him on the spot like that.

Without thinking, she got to her feet and moved over to him. He was stone still, so she straddled his legs and tilted his chin up with her fingertips. "I'm sorry."

"For what?"

"For trying to get you to do something you don't want to do."

His eyes met hers. "I didn't say I don't want to do it."

Sam studied him, tried to process.

"Let's start slow," Logan suggested.

Sam looked over at her husband, saw that he was watching them intently. No way could she not see the interest in his eyes even in the shadows.

"Without the bottle," he added. "If you roll, we take turns doing it to you. If we roll, you perform for us."

Sam nodded and looked back at Elijah. "I'm good with that."

Elijah met her gaze and nodded. "Me, too."

ONE THING LOGAN KNEW ABOUT SAM WAS that she was relentless in her pursuit of what she wanted.

And it was abundantly clear that she was on a mission for a repeat of what had happened this morning.

Logan wouldn't say he was completely on board with the idea, but he wasn't entirely opposed to it, either. He had been shocked by Elijah's touch and definitely not in a bad way. He would go so far as to say he had enjoyed it. It had added an element that had intrigued him, made him come harder than he had in a long damn time. However, if they had planned it, he couldn't say it would've played out the same way. He wasn't sure Sam understood that.

"All right. Who wants to go first?" Sam prompted.

"I think Elijah should," Logan told her. "Then me, then you."

Her pretty lips formed a pout as she got to her feet. Sam retrieved the dice, passed them to Elijah, then grabbed her wineglass and returned to her spot on the floor.

Elijah took a moment to study the dice, turning them in his hands as he read whatever was on them. Logan noticed the smile as it formed and he relaxed a bit.

For most of the day, Elijah had been somewhat standoffish. Since Logan hadn't known what, if anything, he could say to make the situation any less awkward, he'd avoided it altogether, which probably hadn't helped in putting Elijah's mind at ease. And he had to assume that was the reason for the awkward tension. The touching this morning ... no, it hadn't been enough to write home about, but it had been a significant shift for them. Something that Logan was curious to explore, but he wasn't willing to dive right in.

Elijah closed his hand around the dice, shook them, then let them fly down to the floor in front of Sam.

She leaned over and read them. "Lick. Neck." She looked up at Logan. "You call time."

Logan nodded, then watched as she got to her feet and moved back to Elijah, positioning herself on his lap once more.

He smiled to himself when she dramatically tilted Elijah's head to the side so she had better access to the spot she coveted. Logan watched as her little pink tongue dragged over Elijah's skin, and just like anytime the two were intimate, Logan's cock began to swell.

Elijah seemed to relax beneath the onslaught, and it didn't take but a few seconds before Sam was getting into the action, adding some sucking action.

"Stick to the rules," Logan commanded. "Lick, not suck."

She grunted and Elijah chuckled.

"Time."

Sam immediately halted her ministrations, pulling away from Elijah. She grabbed the dice, handed them to Logan with a smirk.

For the next half hour, they each had a handful of turns, Sam having to perform twice as often. If the makers of the game meant this as foreplay, they'd certainly knocked it out of the park. Between stroking nipples, sucking lips, and putting ice below the navel, things had escalated quickly. Enough so, Sam had shed a good portion of her clothing while he and Elijah were wearing only jeans.

"Another beer?" Logan offered Elijah when he finished his last round of kissing Sam's belly.

"Sure."

"I'll take the empty," he offered.

Elijah surprised him, glancing at the empty bottle, then back to Logan. "I think we'll need it for the next round."

Logan stilled, his gaze locked with Elijah's.

This was a major turning point in their relationship. One that, should they pursue it, they would never come back from. And that was what worried Logan the most. He was comfortable with their life together. The three of them. They meshed in a way most people wouldn't understand. Anything more ... well, anything more had the potential to knock over their delicate house of cards.

"If you're good with it," Elijah said softly, still holding his gaze.

"I'm good with it," he admitted, partially surprised that it was the truth.

"Me, too."

Sam's sharp inhale had them both looking her way. "I ... uh ... I think I'll get more wine."

Logan smiled as he realized how badly his wife wanted this to happen.

"I'll add some wood to the fire," Elijah stated, his attention shifting away quickly.

While he did that, Logan went to the kitchen, opened the fridge, and grabbed two more beers. The power was out, but the temperature was holding steady; however, he knew that wouldn't be the case for too long. If they didn't get electricity back soon, there was a good possibility their food would spoil.

But it wasn't something he could worry himself with now. Worst case, they could put it outside to keep it fresh, but he didn't want to point it out and risk Sam getting anxious again.

After opening the bottles, Logan went back to the living room and passed one to Elijah, then returned to his spot on the couch.

Sam was back quickly, downing half her glass before setting it on the table and easing down to her knees.

"Are you cold?" Logan asked, noticing her nipples were hard.

"I'm good." She sounded a bit breathless, which made him smile.

"Whose turn is it?"

"Elijah's," she said, tossing him the dice.

"I'll let you spin the bottle," he said, passing the bottle to Sam.

And this was the point of no return. Introducing that bottle meant they ran the risk of Logan having to perform on Elijah and vice versa. Since the dice held a variety of actions and body parts, there was no telling what it would lead to.

Logan watched as Sam leaned over and placed the bottle on the hardwood floor before spinning it. The anticipation of the moment was obliterated when it landed on Elijah. That helped to settle them as the three of them laughed before Sam did it again. This time it landed on Sam and the rest of the tension dissipated. At least for the moment.

Elijah rolled the dice.

Sam read them. "Warm breath. Below navel."

She smiled as she crawled over to Elijah to complete her task while Logan observed. It was hot, but not as hot as it would've been if Sam had taken Elijah's cock in her mouth. Somehow they'd managed to avoid that particular action although it was a possibility based on the dice. Or at least he assumed that was what the "xxx" referred to.

"Time," he called after allowing it to go on longer than a minute.

Sam huffed, grabbed the dice, and passed them to Logan.

This time, when the bottle stopped spinning, so did Logan's breathing.

Because it landed on Elijah.

Chapter Five

ELIJAH'S HEART THUMPED EXTRA HARD WHEN THE mouth of the bottle landed on him.

He had no idea what those dice would tell him to do, but whatever it was would be something he'd never done before because he would have to perform the action on Logan.

Was he nervous?

Damn straight.

Was he excited?

Surprisingly, yes.

Although he wasn't sure he wanted Logan to know just how much.

Things had been decidedly awkward between them since that morning, and he wasn't sure if it was all him or if Logan was just as freaked out by what had happened. He had tried his best not to make it weird, but no matter how hard he tried, it seemed inevitable. Probably had a lot to do with the fact they hadn't discussed what had happened. Not that he wanted to. Elijah wasn't sure he was ready for that just yet.

Then again, it was all moot because Sam had pulled one of her infamous stunts and managed to manipulate the situation to force it to happen again. And she'd managed to introduce a new game at the same time.

In the beginning, Elijah had been surprised by Sam's games, but over the years he'd gotten used to them, so he hadn't been entirely caught off guard by the idea of this one. Nor with her modified rules.

Didn't change the fact that he wasn't sure how this was going to play out or whether or not it even should. What happened between him and Logan would alter the course of their relationship regardless. Either they would enjoy it and continue down this road or they would enjoy it and not continue. Or, what he prayed *didn't* happen, they would be turned off entirely and things would only go downhill from there.

"Kiss. Lips," Sam announced when Logan tossed the dice to the floor.

Elijah's heart slammed against his ribs once more as he met Logan's gaze.

He had never been one to back down from a challenge, but he'd also never found himself in a position like this.

"I can roll again if you'd like," Logan said, and the way he said it made Elijah realize he was all right with the idea of Elijah kissing him.

"One rule," Elijah stated as he got to his feet and moved toward Logan. "If this gets weird, we talk about it."

"We won't let this destroy us," Logan said firmly.

Elijah nodded, then took a seat beside Logan, their thighs touching.

"Don't move," Elijah said firmly, deciding he was going to be in charge of this moment. Someone needed to be.

Logan remained perfectly still, but the problem came when Elijah found he couldn't move either.

He had never kissed a man before, and while he doubted it would feel much different than kissing a woman, he would *know* it was different. Especially because this was Logan. His stomach pitched and he felt a moment of fear. Elijah did not want to do something that would ultimately ruin what they had. Not even something as innocent as a kiss.

"I can help."

Sam's soft voice drew their attention.

Elijah cocked an eyebrow. "How?"

Her expression was serious when she asked, "Do you trust me?"

"With everything that I am," he said honestly.

She nodded, then got to her feet and came over, positioning herself so she was sitting between them, forcing them both to sit at an angle.

They both turned their attention to her as she got situated. Elijah's breath expelled from his lungs when she leaned in and kissed his mouth. Soft, gentle.

He let her take the reins, giving himself over to her as she licked and sucked at his lower lip, her hand gliding over his bare back. When she pulled back, Elijah realized Logan was watching intently, as he always did.

Sam then performed the same maneuver on Logan while Elijah watched.

It went on for a couple of minutes while they took turns kissing Sam until she'd somehow gotten them closer together.

"I want to watch you kiss him," she whispered in Elijah's ear.

A jolt of heat speared him. Her words were a sensual seduction, and although he was far more dominant in the bedroom than Sam, he found he wanted to please her by doing as she requested.

Without thinking, Elijah leaned over and pressed his lips to Logan's. They both hesitated briefly, a brush of lips and nothing more.

Sam shifted and Elijah felt her hand on the back of his head as though she was holding him in place. It wasn't necessary because he wasn't moving away. No, he was rooted to the sofa, to the moment, trying to remember how to breathe.

"Don't stop," Logan grumbled, his hand sliding onto Elijah's thigh.

That single command was enough to have Elijah going in for the kill. He crushed his mouth to Logan's and gave himself over to the kiss. He let the sensations overwhelm him, the feel of Logan's firm lips, his tongue, the whiskers on his cheeks. Elijah didn't hesitate to see whether Logan welcomed him because he didn't have to. Logan growled low in his throat and pulled Elijah into him.

The kiss was earth-scorching hot, unlike anything Elijah had ever experienced. There was a definite difference between kissing Sam and kissing Logan. Not only because of their gender but also because of their personalities. Sam was generously submissive while Logan was fully dominating. They were at war for supremacy as their tongues dueled, hands groping.

Elijah had no idea how long it went on. It lasted until Sam moaned, her soft, cool hands caressing his back, pulling him out of the moment.

"Christ Almighty," Logan whispered.

Sam's eyes were wide as she stared between them, as though she was waiting for one of them to do something.

Elijah wiped his lower lip with his thumb as he met Logan's gaze again.

Now for the moment of truth.

SAM WAS TRANSFIXED BY THE SIGHT OF Logan and Elijah looking at one another.

It was like watching two hungry wolves who'd gone head-to-head for their meal, and somehow they'd both come out the victor.

"Fuck," Elijah mumbled, his chest heaving.

That had been…

Unbelievable.

Freaking hot.

Sinful.

Sam wanted to watch them again, wanted to see her men give in to whatever this urge was to devour one another, but she knew better than to make the request. She wasn't in charge of this, no matter how much she wished that were the case. They had to find common ground for this to move forward. If, in fact, it was going to move forward.

"Enough games," Logan said, his gaze swinging to Sam.

She wasn't about to argue, but even if she had been, he gave her no time to do so.

Before she knew what was happening, Logan and Elijah were on their feet. A second later, Logan had her tossed over his shoulder and was marching toward the stairs. She squealed but remained still, not wanting him to drop her on his path to what she hoped was a bedroom.

Seemingly picking one at random, Logan strolled in and tossed Sam to the bed, making her laugh. It died off quickly when Logan stripped off the remainder of his clothes, then reached for her panties and jerked them down her legs. Elijah wasn't far behind, strolling into the room looking just as dangerous, his eyes flashing with heat.

"Don't move," Logan ordered her before looking at Elijah. "Start a fire? I'll get the lube."

Sam shivered but it had nothing to do with the chill in the room and everything to do with what she knew Logan had in store for her.

She held her breath, watched as Logan disappeared into the bathroom and Elijah went over to start a fire in the fireplace in the bedroom. She wasn't sure they were going to need the added heat just yet, but she wouldn't complain, especially since the room was almost completely dark now that night was falling.

"This is your doing," Logan said firmly when he strolled out of the bathroom. "You got what you wanted and now we're gonna get what we want."

Oh, boy. She loved that edge in his voice. He was in true alpha mode.

"Which is?" she taunted, her gaze drifting to Elijah as he stood tall before stripping off his jeans and joining her on the bed.

Logan didn't answer, but she wasn't waiting for it because Elijah's mouth crushed to hers as he rolled them so that she was on top of him.

"Put my cock inside you," he rasped, gripping her hair.

Sam reached between them and found his cock hard and thick. She stroked him once, twice before guiding him right where she needed him. He didn't allow her to ease down on him, though. Elijah gripped her hips and pulled her down, making her cry out as the ecstasy of pleasure/pain washed over her. She loved when he was rough, when he took what he wanted, when he was so overcome by his own desires that he took his pleasure from her.

She was vaguely aware of Logan moving around behind her, but she let Elijah distract her. With her hands planted on his chest, she rode him, rolling her hips and fucking him as though her life depended on it.

"Fucking tight," Elijah groaned, his eyes locked on her face.

"She's about to be tighter," Logan said from behind her.

Sam leaned forward when Logan's big hand landed in the center of her back. She didn't fight him, giving in because she loved when they did this. When they overwhelmed her, when they lost control. And they had lost control, there was no doubt about it.

When Logan shifted closer, Elijah stilled her with a firm grip on her hips. He lifted his head to get to her mouth and she succumbed to the kiss, lying out over him. Strong hands gripped her butt cheeks, separating them. Cool lube dripped over her rear entrance, followed by a finger being inserted.

Sam tried to rock against the intrusion, welcoming it because she was on fire and she needed them to quench this inexplicable need. Watching them kiss had done something to her, unraveled her in a way she hadn't expected.

Logan groaned and then she felt the blunt head of his cock as he pressed against her hole. Elijah's tongue slowed, sliding against hers as he breathed her in.

"Tell him you like it," Elijah urged. "That you like having him fuck your ass."

"I *love* it," she whimpered, shifting so she could take him deeper. "I love the two of you inside me at the same time."

Sam could still remember the first time she'd taken Elijah and Logan at the same time. They had both fucked her pussy and it had been an experience she had never forgotten. Since then, they'd experimented in so many ways. But having them like this … there was something carnal about it. It made her feel alive in a way she couldn't explain. Sam loved when they double-teamed her because she felt so close to them both.

Logan's hands gripped her hips and she realized Elijah's were still there, too. Together they held her in place while Logan penetrated her asshole, Elijah fucking her pussy. In and out, they alternated, slowly at first. It wasn't long before they had their rhythm, and they began plowing into her, sensation after sensation consuming her entire body. Her skin felt too tight as heat engulfed her. A ball of electricity formed deep within her, and the next thing she knew, it detonated and she was soaring, her insides humming as her muscles tensed, letting the energy of her orgasm consume her.

"Fuck," Elijah shouted, his hips bucking upward as he stilled, buried deep inside her.

Logan growled, obviously following their lead as he rammed her backside, the two of them coming together.

Sam wasn't sure what this meant for the three of them, where things would go from here, but she knew without a doubt that she was looking forward to letting it play out, just like Logan had advised.

Making the Most of It

Hunter, Kye, and Dani from *Tomorrow's Too Late*

Hunter agreed to a protection detail three days before
Christmas. See how Dani and Kye make the most of it when
Hunter gets snowed in.

Monday, December 20, 2021

"IT'S JUST FOR THREE DAYS," HUNTER KOGAN told his wife. "I promise, I'll be home in time for all the festivities."

Dani stared up at him, her golden-brown eyes glittering skeptically. "Promise?"

He smiled and pressed a kiss to her mouth. "Promise."

"I'm holding you to that," she said firmly, turning and strolling out of their bedroom.

Hunter finished tossing a few things in his bag. The job was an easy one, which was the only reason he'd signed up for it. Protect a Saudi prince for three days, during which he had a handful of public events he needed to attend. Hunter had done this type of assignment a million times, and during the holidays, he found it best to step out from behind the desk he rode most of the year to help out. It was one of the few concessions he'd made when agreeing to step into the management role alongside Ryan Trexler.

"Who's goin' with you?"

Hunter glanced over at the doorway to see Kye standing there, shoulder pressed to the jamb.

"Deck," he answered, referring to Decker Bromwell, one of Sniper 1 Security's many tenured security agents.

Kye nodded. "He's good to have on your six."

"He'll do," Hunter said, zipping his bag. He would've preferred to have Kye on his six, but it hadn't been an option. Plus, Hunter preferred at least one of them was home with Dani when the other was on assignment. He hated to think about her being home alone despite the fact she was constantly assuring him she could take care of herself.

"Your tux bein' delivered?" Kye asked when Hunter shouldered his bag.

"Yeah. They'll be waitin' for me at the hotel."

"They?" Kye chuckled.

Hunter glared. He hated the penguin suits, and this time he would be wearing one for three days in a row, hence the reason he needed more than one.

"Well, have a safe trip."

Hunter stopped in front of Kye. "I'll do my best," he said before leaning in and pressing a kiss to his mouth. "You better think about me while I'm gone."

"Bet on it," Kye answered, nipping Hunter's bottom lip.

It was all he could do not to throw Kye on the bed and have his wicked way with the man. Somehow he managed to refrain.

He found Dani in the kitchen, planted a kiss on her sweet lips, and then disappeared out the door.

Three days, that was all it was. He'd be home well in time for Christmas.

Thursday, December 23, 2021

"SON OF A MOTHER—" HUNTER BIT OFF the retort before a string of curse words could escape.

He could not believe that he was stranded in a fucking airport hotel of all places.

Two fucking days before Christmas.

Tossing his bag on the bed, he let the door slam shut behind him. He and Deck had lucked out in that they could find a hotel room at all. He figured it had something to do with the fact the Sniper 1 teams had stayed in this particular establishment plenty of times over the years. The least they could do was lock down a couple of rooms for them for emergencies. However, it truly was a miracle considering most of the flights out of JFK had been grounded due to the storm that was wreaking havoc on the Northeast.

So here he was, grateful as fuck that at least there were *two* rooms left. He wasn't sure he could've survived spending even one night with Deck as a roommate. The guy was a damn good agent, but he was annoying as shit.

He needed to call Dani and Kye and give them the bad news. He knew she was not going to be happy with him, but Hunter hoped that if he promised to move heaven and earth tomorrow and get home before dinnertime, she'd forgive him.

Hunter strolled toward the window to pull open the curtains when his cell phone buzzed in his pocket.

Pulling it out, he glanced at the screen, noticed it was a FaceTime call. There was only one person who preferred to talk to him face-to-face and thank God for that. Hunter was not a fan of seeing people on the phone. It was just weird.

Because he couldn't ignore them, he tapped the button to answer, hating the image of himself that appeared.

"Please tell me your flight wasn't grounded," Dani said as soon as the connection went through.

Hunter exhaled heavily and fell into the stiff upholstered chair near the window. Just outside the window, the snow was falling heavily, getting thicker by the minute.

"No such luck, baby," he told her, turning the camera so she would get a view of the snowfall.

When he turned back, she was frowning. The pout that appeared on her mouth was sexy as hell, and it went a long way to improving his mood. Not because she was likely genuinely upset but because he knew that pout. She was in payback mode.

"I figured you'd be in bed by now," he said, watching her on the screen. He could tell by the way she was holding it that she wasn't talking to him on her phone but rather her iPad, which she preferred to use whenever she was at home.

"We were waiting up for you."

"Yeah, well..." He sighed again. "I won't be home tonight. And I'll be lucky if we can get outta here tomorrow. This storm's a bad one."

This was what he got for banking on being home for Christmas.

"Where's Kye?" he asked, watching the screen as Dani moved from one room to another, lights clicking off as she went.

Hunter could make out the bedroom when she flipped on the bedside lamp.

"He's in the shower." She moved again, this time dropping onto the bed, the headboard appearing behind her head.

"Yeah?" Hunter couldn't deny the stirring that occurred in his jeans when he thought about Kye getting out of the shower and joining Dani in that big bed of theirs.

"Mmm-hmmm."

"Does he know you're callin' me?"

She shook her head and there was an unmistakable twinkle in her eye. He recognized it and his cock kicked in his jeans.

"If all goes well, I might be able to catch a flight out tomorrow afternoon," he said conversationally, waiting to see what his feisty wife had in store for him.

"Let's hope so." Her tone held a hint of an edge and Hunter knew she wasn't happy with him. She'd been against him taking this job in the first place, so it was only fair that she was upset that he might not be home for Christmas.

Before he could apologize for choosing work, Hunter heard Kye's voice in the background. A second later, the camera angle shifted from Dani to a very naked man strolling toward the bed.

"You called him, huh?" Kye chuckled, grinning at the phone screen.

"I did," she said, her voice coming from off screen.

"You better not miss Christmas," Kye warned. "I'm not sure she'll forgive you for that."

"Probably not."

"Come here," Dani instructed, again, her voice off screen.

"What are you two up to?" Hunter asked, watching with anticipation as the camera angle shifted down from Kye's handsome face, over his sculpted chest, his spectacular abs and...

Oh, yeah. The man was most definitely naked. Gloriously naked. And fucking hard.

"Holy fuck," Hunter murmured when he saw that Kye's hand was fisting his thick, rigid cock, stroking in that slow, teasing way of his.

The camera shifted back to Dani's face. She smiled. "We're making the most of it."

"Making the most of what?"

"You being gone."

"Is that right?"

"Yep."

There was some dizzying movement for a moment, and then the iPad was set up on the nightstand, giving Hunter an unobstructed view of their bed.

A second later, Kye was reclining back on it and Hunter's breath lodged deep in his throat.

Kye had known the instant he stepped out of the bathroom that their wife was about to do something very, very naughty.

He'd long ago learned to take his cues from her, and ever since she received Hunter's text message that their flight was possibly going to get cancelled, Dani had been in a mood. It just so happened that she wasn't the sort to get angry. More so she liked to get even.

And apparently, getting even with Hunter for scheduling a last-minute work trip right before Christmas meant giving the man a live show.

Kye peered over at the iPad, which was propped up, and Hunter's handsome face was on the screen. He was watching intently, clearly waiting to see what their wife was going to do next. He found it interesting that she'd opted for the bigger screen rather than her phone, but as he watched Hunter gritting his teeth, Kye understood why. This was a much better view for them.

"Eyes over here," Dani said in a raspy voice that had Kye's attention instantly shifting from the iPad to the sexy woman who was now straddling his hips.

She was wearing one of Hunter's flannel button-downs and evidently nothing beneath it.

Sexy as fuck.

"Your only job is to make sure that husband of ours can see everything that I'm doing," Dani informed him, holding his gaze.

Kye nodded, but his gaze shifted lower when she began to slowly unbutton the shirt, revealing her lovely cleavage. "I'll do my best."

When she revealed one breast, he sucked in air.

When the other appeared, Kye moaned.

"Holy fuck," Hunter said from the iPad.

Dani's attention shifted to Hunter as she let the shirt slide off her shoulders. "Do you wish you hadn't taken the job?"

Hunter's response was immediate. "I didn't have much of a choice."

Kye kept his eyes on his wife's tits, grinning. That definitely wasn't what Dani had expected him to say.

Dani grabbed Kye's hands and lifted them to her breasts. She didn't have to give him any instructions after that because Kye knew exactly what she liked. He plumped her breasts and pinched her nipples, all the while listening to Hunter's breaths growing more labored on the call.

She remained in control, though, leaning forward and dangling one breast over his mouth. Kye latched on with his teeth, nipping lightly until she moaned.

"Dani … baby…" Hunter groaned.

"Now do you wish you hadn't taken the job?" she repeated.

This time he didn't answer but Kye was too busy sucking on Dani's tit to care.

What Hunter probably couldn't see was the way Kye was rolling his hips, sliding his cock through Dani's slick folds. He knew she was doing this to torment him, and he loved her all the more for it.

Dani shifted, her breast falling from between his lips. Her mouth descended on Kye's briefly, and the kiss that ensued was hot enough to spark flames.

Oh, yeah, she was definitely out to punish Hunter and she was going to use Kye in the process.

Lucky, lucky him.

"You're gonna need to shift the camera," Dani said when her lips trailed down over his chin.

It took him a minute to process what she was saying as her mouth moved lower, over his chest, his abs...

"Goddammit, Kye, you better let me see," Hunter growled.

Kye reached over with one free hand, angling the iPad so Hunter had a view of their wife as she took Kye's cock in her mouth.

"Fuck," he growled at the same time Hunter said, "Suck him, Dani."

Kye felt the shiver that raced through her, knew she loved when Hunter dominated their lovemaking. It was a frequent occurrence, something they both found immensely hot.

Dani was relentless, working him like a pro, her hand curled around the base of his shaft, stroking in tandem with her bobbing mouth.

"Show me," Hunter demanded.

Dani pulled her mouth from him, holding Kye's cock firmly so Hunter had an up-close view of the slick, swollen head and the pre-cum that was continuing to pool there.

"Now do you wish you hadn't taken the job?" Dani asked.

"I didn't have a choice," Hunter said again, clearly on to her game. He was going to continue to deny her until she gave him everything he wanted.

"Let me see your cock," Dani insisted.

Kye's gaze shot to the iPad as Hunter moved his camera, revealing the thick purple shaft he was stroking in his big fist. From how hard he was, Hunter was definitely enjoying the show.

Not for the first time, Kye wished the man was there with them.

"Stroke it," Dani commanded.

Hunter grunted, but his hand stroked slowly, surely over the velvet-smooth flesh.

Jesus. This was by far one of their most erotic encounters and that was saying something.

"I want you to ride him," Hunter said roughly, the camera returning to his face. "I want to see everything."

As far as Kye was concerned, they were putting him in a precarious situation. Who could expect him to control the camera angle when their wife was riding his cock?

"Show me, Kye," Hunter rumbled.

Kye nodded because he couldn't find his voice. Dani had shifted and was straddling him, up on her knees as she angled his cock to her hot, wet center. He managed to turn the iPad, hoping that Hunter could see but not all that worried in that moment. No, Kye's brain cells were obliterated as he watched the sexiest woman in the world as she sank down on him, taking his cock inch by inch.

"God, yes," Dani moaned, her hands shifting to her breasts as she kneaded them roughly.

And then she was riding him, rocking her hips, taking him in deep, retreating slowly.

"I'm gonna come while you're fucking him," Hunter declared. "And when I do, I want you to come. I better hear you, Dani."

Kye didn't care that they were using him for their own personal gain. Hell, he fucking loved that they were.

"Ah, Jesus," Kye cried out when Dani's muscles locked down on him as she began to bounce on his dick.

"Fuck, yes," Hunter bellowed. "You both better come."

For several minutes, the only sound was their labored breaths and strangled moans as the three of them raced toward climax.

As instructed, they managed to hold off until Hunter bellowed loudly. Dani followed right over, her pussy clamping down like a vise, milking Kye's release from him.

"What about now?" Dani asked, panting as she fell forward on Kye.

Hunter chuckled softly. "Baby, I've regretted it from the minute I walked out the door. But I promise you, I'll be home as soon as I can."

"You better," she said, her head turned toward the camera, ear pressed to Kye's chest. "In the meantime, we'll continue to make the most of it."

Oh, yes, they certainly would.

The Perfect Gift

Wolfe, Rhys, and Amy from *Hard to Hold*

Wolfe and Rhys have been working on a gift for Amy for months. With only days left to finish it, they're getting creative about how to keep it a secret.

Thursday, December 23, 2021

WOLFE CAINE STOOD IN THE WAREHOUSE, HIS belt sander in hand as he studied the piece of furniture he'd been working on for the past two weeks.

What should've taken him a couple of days had dragged out for far longer than necessary, but it was almost complete, which meant they were so close to finishing Amy's Christmas present.

So fucking close.

It hadn't been an easy process considering he'd built every piece with his own two hands. A process that was made nearly impossible considering she worked with him here at the furniture store and was in the building day in and day out. There were times when Wolfe had felt like a cheating spouse. A man sneaking around on the woman he loved, avoiding her catching him in the act. All so he could ensure she didn't catch a glimpse of what he was doing. He honest to God could not fathom how anyone would want to endure that much stress simply so they could step out on someone. It was nerve-racking.

For the record, he wasn't fond of being sneaky.

Luckily, Rhys had helped out, keeping their wife occupied on the weekends so Wolfe could get in a few extra hours of work here at the shop. Although he didn't care for the idea of leaving Rhys and Amy on their days off—it was rare when the three of them had a day off together—he knew it would be worth it in the end. Now that Christmas was two days away, he was putting the finishing touches on it, and then the only thing left was getting it moved to the house and installed.

All without Amy figuring it out.

He exhaled heavily, set the sander down, and brushed the sawdust from his arms.

The squeak of the main door on its hinges had Wolfe spinning around, stepping in front of the piece of furniture as though he could possibly shield it from Amy in the event she was the one coming in the door.

He let out a relieved sigh when he saw who it was.

"What the hell're you doin' here? I thought we were shuttin' down for the week?"

Wolfe glanced at his cousin then turned back to survey his project. "Just puttin' the finishing touches on Amy's stuff."

"Oh, right," Lynx said, a smile in his voice as he approached. "You almost done?"

"Just about. Need to install it so we can paint."

"Need help?"

Wolfe grinned at Lynx. "Thought you'd never ask."

It had only taken a few minutes to call Rhys and get him to take Amy out to lunch and for some last-minute shopping so he and Lynx could carry the pieces he'd been working on to the house. After putting his muscles to good use loading and unloading the truck, then hefting the furniture into the house, they were able to get everything set up in the attic space that Wolfe and Rhys had been working to convert for Amy.

Because their wife worked so hard day in and day out and still refused to go out and about—the years she'd spent in hiding had done a number on her—they had decided they would build her the ultimate retreat. A space just for her right there in the safety and comfort of her own home.

"What do you think?" Wolfe asked Lynx when they got the last piece set up.

"She's gonna go apeshit," he said with a laugh.

Wolfe doubted that, but he appreciated his cousin's sentiment.

It had taken some effort for him and Rhys to decide what they would get Amy this year. She wasn't much into material items, so they'd learned to get creative. She preferred to pick out her own clothing and she didn't care much for jewelry, so those were never an option. Kitchen appliances were always a good idea, except they'd bought her nearly one of everything in the past couple of years. Books were a must, but Amy preferred to read on her electronic reader thing, so she generally took care of that.

But it was the last one that had given him and Rhys the idea of creating a reading space just for her. A place she could get comfortable and not be bothered by them.

"Need help paintin'?" Lynx offered.

Wolfe narrowed his gaze, focusing on his cousin. While Lynx was usually around in the event Wolfe needed help, the man wasn't ever quite this forthcoming with his assistance.

"What're you up to?" he asked suspiciously.

"Nothin'," he answered quickly.

Too quickly.

Lynx barked a laugh. "Fine. Rhys offered to pay me to help out. Said you'd need it since y'all both can't work on it at the same time."

Wolfe should've figured.

"In that case…"

Wolfe grabbed the paint cans they'd stashed a week ago, along with the rollers and pans, and shoved one in Lynx's direction.

If they were lucky, they'd get it finished before Amy and Rhys got back.

And if they didn't … well, he'd have to deal with that when the time came.

"I STILL CAN'T BELIEVE YOU WERE WILLING to come to the mall two days before Christmas."

Rhys peered at Amy, smiled. Truth was, he didn't have much of a choice. Wolfe had insisted he get Amy out of the house and there weren't many options at the moment.

"Figured it's better to be safe than sorry," he lied. Rhys had already ensured they had gotten gifts for everyone on their list, and he'd doubled-checked it a few times to make sure he hadn't missed anyone. Anything they bought today, which they undoubtedly would do, would be overkill.

But hey, if it meant giving Wolfe time to put the finishing touches on Amy's gift, then he was willing to suffer with the best of them.

"If you don't mind, I'd like to go to Bath and Body Works," Amy suggested. "There's something Reagan mentioned she saw. Thought I'd get it for her."

With Amy's hand in his, he let her lead the way.

Two hours later, they'd accomplished the not-so-easy feat of dealing with holiday shoppers. Rhys was loaded down with bags full of more gifts than anyone knew what to do with. Thankfully, Amy had allowed him to pay the people sitting in the mall to wrap the presents so they wouldn't have to. It'd been a good way to waste another hour.

However, Rhys couldn't stall forever without making Amy suspicious, so when she suggested she was ready to go this last time, he indulged her. Using the ruse he was checking on things at the station, Rhys shot Wolfe a quick text letting him know they'd be home in half an hour. The message he got back didn't inspire confidence, but he let it go, hoping against hope that Wolfe would do his best to get things cleaned up.

"Anything you need to deal with?"

Rhys's gaze shot to Amy. "What?"

She nodded at his phone. "Work? Something you need to do?"

He sighed, put his phone down in the center console, and started the truck. "Nah. It's all good."

Amy chuckled. "I figured as much."

As he pulled the truck out of the parking lot, he glanced over at the woman he loved beyond measure. The mischievous smile curving her mouth had his insides tightening.

"Why? Somethin' you'd like to do at the station?"

"Maybe." Her cheeks turned a pretty shade of pink.

For the past year or so, Rhys had noticed she was getting bolder, requesting things she hadn't originally requested. Sexual things. Dirty things. Back when the three of them had first gotten together, Wolfe was generally the one to instigate their intimate moments, but as time went by, Amy had been making her desires known.

He wasn't complaining by any means. In fact, Rhys enjoyed reaping the benefits of having two lovers.

"We can stop by there if you'd like," Amy said softly, her attention out the window.

Christ, just thinking about where her mind might go with that suggestion made his dick hard.

"Perhaps we'll swing by," he told her. "I think there might be some … uh … forms that need my attention."

Amy giggled, her attention remaining out the window. "I think so, too."

AMY WAS NO DUMMY. SHE KNEW WOLFE and Rhys were up to something. Had been for a few months now. For goodness' sakes, Rhys was willing to go to the mall just two days before Christmas in order to distract her, which told her only one thing: whatever they were up to had something to do with her.

Which was the very reason she hadn't put too much effort into figuring it out.

Not because she didn't want to know. Oh, she most certainly did. Amy was curious like that and she enjoyed figuring out the puzzles. However, she realized they were going to extremes to hide it, and due to the timing, she had figured it was something pertaining to Christmas. So for their sakes, she hadn't pushed or snooped, wanting whatever it was to be a surprise.

Of course, she could be completely off and whatever they were up to had nothing to do with her at all. If that was the case, she would be giving them shit when the time came, but for now, she was keeping her cool.

"It won't take but a minute," Rhys told her, pulling up to the station and shutting off the truck. "If you wanna come in."

Amy grinned to herself, then hopped out of the truck.

Rhys was waiting for her at the front of the truck. Like he always did, he linked his fingers with hers and led the way into the building.

"Hey, Sheriff," Chip greeted around a mouthful of what appeared to be a sub sandwich.

"Not here for long," Rhys told the deputy, leading Amy down the hall, barely giving her enough time to offer a quick hello and a wave.

Chip was chuckling behind them when Rhys pulled her around the corner and down the narrow hall that led to his private office.

Realizing Chip would know what they were doing, Amy felt her cheeks warm, but she ignored the heat of embarrassment. So what if he knew? She was a grown woman and ... and ... and she was in a long-term committed relationship with Rhys. If they wanted to sneak into his office and have sex, by God, they could do that.

Yep, now the tips of her ears were hot.

Not that they did it often. The sex in his office thing.

That was a lie.

They did it often.

Really, really often.

What it was about being in his office, Amy didn't know. Maybe it was the fact that others might figure out what they were doing, but they all respected the sheriff too much to call them out on it. Amy realized she liked living dangerously. Like this, anyway. Not the real danger that she'd finally managed to claw her way out from under.

The click of the door closing brought her out of her thoughts just in time to let out a shriek when Rhys spun her around and pressed her back to the door.

"You like teasin' me, don't you?"

She grinned against his mouth. "Who said I was teasing?"

In a bold move, she pressed the back of her hand against the fly of his jeans, loving the fact that he was already hard. It was a powerful thing to know she could do that to him. Him *and* Wolfe. Her men were not shy in showing her just what she did to them.

"And just what did you have in mind?" Rhys asked, pulling his mouth from hers.

Amy was breathless from the passion in his kiss, but she managed a smile even as she slid down the door until she was crouching before him.

Rhys planted one hand on the wood, staring down at her, watching but not moving.

She knew he was going to make her work for it. They enjoyed doing that. Forcing her to own up to her boldness, to follow through with what she wanted.

Drawing on every ounce of that confidence, Amy reached for the button on his jeans, then for the zipper. Within seconds, she had his erection freed, the heat of him filling her palm as she stroked softly.

Rhys groaned low in his throat, those blue eyes pinned on her.

Amy loved when he watched her. There was so much reverence in his gaze. That mixed with an abundance of passion always made her feel like the most beautiful woman in the world.

Teasing him, Amy licked the swollen head, waited for the rugged groan that would follow. When it did, she stopped teasing, taking him into her mouth. Slowly, she slid her tongue along his shaft as she hollowed her cheeks and pulled him in deep. There was no denying she had a sensitive gag reflex, but Amy had learned to work him in a way that seemed to please.

"Fuck's sake," he growled softly. "Your mouth … fuckin' heaven."

Amy's insides tingled, her pussy clenching, eager for him to fill her. She craved Rhys and Wolfe in ways she honestly didn't understand. Before her path had crossed with Wolfe and Rhys, Amy had hated sex. Hated what it even stood for. There were times she had even imagined life without it. She had never worried she wouldn't be fulfilled.

Then she met them and her thought process had changed.

No, *she* had changed. They filled her life with light and laughter and ultimately eradicated the dark cloud she'd been living under. They were her salvation and she craved them.

She continued on her path to blow Rhys's mind, leaving it up to him to tell her when he couldn't take any more. When Rhys's big hand slid into her hair, she knew it wouldn't be long.

He gripped her hair in his fist, halting her ministrations but not pulling her up.

"I don't wanna come like this," he said softly, probably ensuring no one else could hear them.

Rhys's gaze shifted over his shoulder for a moment, and the next thing Amy knew, he was helping her to her feet. Then she was bent over his desk and he was behind her, sliding her leggings and panties down like a man starved for her.

Heat flashed through every nerve ending, her body trembling with the sort of desire she had a difficult time containing. She loved the way he manhandled her as though he couldn't wait another second to have her.

As she lay across his desk, Amy was shackled by the cotton around her ankles, but that didn't stop Rhys. He slid his hand between her legs, his fingers gliding through her slick folds. It was her turn to moan.

"You're ready for me."

Amy noticed it wasn't a question. Then again, there weren't many times when she wasn't ready for either of her men. It was as though they kept her in this heightened state of arousal just for moments like this.

"Widen your knees for just a second," he instructed.

Amy did, gripping the edge of the desk with her fingers as the blunt head of his cock pressed against her opening.

She swallowed a moan as he slid in deep, the friction making her nipples tighten.

"Close your knees."

Amy did, which created a tightness that she knew Rhys enjoyed.

And then he was fucking her, one hand planted on her back to hold her in place, the other on her hip as he thrust. She was at his mercy, shackled by her clothing, but it was sheer perfection.

Or it would've been if she could've cried out. Instead, Amy had to focus on choking back her moans as the pleasure intensified. She held on for as long as she could, but Rhys obliterated her control when he reached beneath her and found her clit with his skilled finger. Within seconds she was rocketing to the peak. She barely managed to hold back the sound as her orgasm crested, shattering her.

"Oh, fuck, yes," Rhys bit out, his voice low. "You're so fucking tight like this. Oh, fuck … Amy…"

He slammed into her one final time and came before leaning over her and pressing a kiss to her cheek.

"You're a naughty, naughty girl, you know that?"

She chuckled softly. "I'm trying."

Saturday, December 25, 2021

WOLFE WOKE UP ON CHRISTMAS DAY TO find he was alone in bed.

It was rare for Rhys and Amy to get up before him, much less slip out before he was roused enough to stop them, but last night had been a long night. He'd had to wait until Amy fell asleep on the couch when they'd been watching *Elf* before he could put the final touches on her gift. Rhys had stuck it out with him, but they'd taken turns ensuring she didn't wake up and catch them.

He rolled over, listened for sounds that would alert him to where they were.

From the kitchen, he heard the familiar clink of silverware and glassware, which meant someone was making breakfast.

From the bathroom, he heard the shower water running, which meant one of them was in there.

It was anyone's guess who was where, but lucky for Wolfe, it didn't matter to him which of them he encountered. That was one of the benefits of being with two people he loved more than anything. He was eager for both of them and he would not be disappointed either way.

Forcing himself up, he gripped his cock in his hand, the damn thing standing at full mast and growing harder by the second.

When a throat cleared from the bathroom, he smiled.

Well, that settled that. Rhys was the one in the shower.

Without making a sound, Wolfe waltzed into the bathroom, then right into the shower.

"You're not nearly as silent as you think you are," Rhys grumbled as the water sprayed over his face.

"I didn't realize it was a contest," he said, pressing his chest to Rhys's back and then kissing his neck. "Mornin'."

"Merry Christmas."

"It is very merry, isn't it?" Wolfe asked, reaching around and finding Rhys's cock and stroking slowly.

"Lemme guess, this is my gift?" Rhys laughed.

"Depends on how you look at it." Wolfe squeezed Rhys's dick more firmly, earning a rumbling groan in return. "Might be *my* gift."

"Is that right?"

When Rhys relaxed back against him, Wolfe pressed his hips forward, slipping his cock along the crack of Rhys's ass.

"Your ass or your mouth," Wolfe rasped against Rhys's neck. "I want one or the other."

Rhys answered by pressing his hips back and groaning.

"I do love fuckin' you first thing in the mornin'," Wolfe said, pulling back so he could grab the bottle of lube they kept in the shower.

Seconds later, he was sliding deep inside the man he loved, pressing his hand between Rhys's shoulder blades to urge him forward. When he was positioned so Wolfe had the traction he needed, he impaled Rhys.

"Fuck."

"Hurt?"

"Uh-uh. Fuck me, Wolfe. Now."

He gave his man what he asked for, alternating between slow, shallow strokes and fast, deep ones. He couldn't waste time though since he knew breakfast would be ready soon, but damn, he had to savor at least for a little while. A minute.

Three.

Five.

Fuck, he wasn't going to last that damn long.

"You close?" he asked, curling his hand over Rhys's shoulder to hold him still while Rhys was jerking his own cock furiously.

"Yeah ... fuck..."

Wolfe gripped Rhys's hips with both hands and drilled him again and again until they were both panting and moaning. When Rhys's guttural cry echoed in the bathroom, Wolfe followed him right over.

AMY HEARD SOUNDS COMING FROM THE BEDROOM, so she went to see what was keeping her men. Rhys had said he was grabbing a shower and would wake Wolfe up afterward. Since her men took the fastest showers in the history of water pressure, it shouldn't have taken them this long, which, if she was right, could only mean one thing. They'd gotten sidetracked.

No sooner did she step into the bedroom than she realized what the holdup was. The rough grunts and moans echoing off the shower tile told her all she needed to know.

Rather than interrupt their morning sex-capade, Amy grinned as she returned to the kitchen. She set out their plates and put the food on the table so they could dish up what they wanted. She knew Wolfe loved her biscuits and gravy, so she'd doubled up on the sausage she put in it just for him. And since Rhys was more of an eggs and toast guy, she'd made him a skillet of scrambled eggs and a stack of bread. She never knew how hungry they would be, but she suspected they'd be hungrier since their rendezvous in the shower.

She was pouring them coffee when they both strolled out of the bedroom, dressed in sweats and T-shirts, their preferred staying-in-bed-all-day clothes.

At least they were wearing clothes.

"Mornin'," Wolfe greeted, grabbing Amy from behind and pressing a kiss to her cheek.

She smiled at him over her shoulder. "Morning. Ready to eat?"

"Only if you wanna wait on opening your presents," he responded.

"If I hadn't worked so hard on this, I'd say to hold off," she admitted. "But…" Amy motioned for them to sit down.

Rhys pulled out her chair and waited for her to ease into it before he took his spot at her side. Wolfe started to sit but halted before making a beeline for the refrigerator.

"What are you doing?" she asked, watching curiously. "I've got the orange juice over here."

He rummaged through the top shelf, moving things around and over before evidently finding what he was looking for. He grabbed a bowl out of the cabinet, then did something that she couldn't see because he was blocking her view. When he returned to the table with the bowl, Amy watched as he set it down.

She was pretty sure her heart skipped a beat right after it swelled to overflowing. The bowl held strawberries and grapes on one half and what looked suspiciously like her favorite fruit dip—which was homemade—on the other.

"Did you make this yourself?"

"With a little help," Wolfe said, glancing at Rhys as he took a seat.

There were many days when she didn't think her heart could be any fuller than it already was. And then one or both of them would do something like this and she was surprised to find that her heart could grow even bigger.

Rhys couldn't recall the last time he'd eaten so much.

Over the years, Amy had become a phenomenal cook, learning new things all the time. He certainly wasn't surprised. Amy was good at everything she did. Smart, beautiful, witty. She'd come out of her shell since they'd taken down the bastard who had tormented her, keeping her as a prisoner in her own home, under his thumb. They were lucky to have her, that was for damn sure.

As though he'd been waiting for Rhys to finish, Wolfe tossed down his fork, letting it clatter on his empty plate, and announced, "All right, time for presents."

Rhys smiled, looked at Amy, back to Wolfe. He was honestly surprised Wolfe had been able to wait this long. Patience was not the man's strong suit.

"I get to go first," Amy declared.

Rhys could see the disappointment in Wolfe's eyes. The man was so eager to give her their gift he could hardly contain himself.

"Fine," Wolfe conceded. "You go first."

Amy stood and reached for her plate to carry to the sink.

"I'll get that in a little while," Rhys informed her. "You cooked; we'll clean."

"But first presents," Wolfe said, sounding more impatient than just a second ago.

Rhys chuckled, taking Amy's hand. "Come on. Before he explodes."

Amy laughed, giving in and letting him lead her to the couch.

The Christmas tree was lit, the colorful lights twinkling, the rainbow of colored ornaments reflecting the light. They left the decorating up to Amy because they'd learned she wanted a different theme every year, and who were they to stand in her way? Last year had been a blue and silver theme; the year before was red and gold. This year she'd gone all out with multicolored lights and glass ornaments covering the tree.

No sooner had Rhys sat down than Wolfe launched to his feet again. "Nope. Can't do it."

"Can't do what?" Amy sounded sincerely worried.

Wolfe held out his hand to her. "Come on. You get your gift first."

Amy glanced at Rhys, eyebrows angled down as though she was worried.

He couldn't help it, he laughed. "I knew this was gonna happen. Might as well let him go first."

"Yes, let me go first," Wolfe insisted, tugging her to her feet.

Rhys stood, followed them to the small hallway that held the attic stairs that Wolfe was already pulling down from the ceiling.

"What's going on?" Amy asked, her tone losing its humor.

"Don't worry," Rhys assured her. "It's nothing nefarious."

She didn't look convinced, but she did finally follow Wolfe up into the attic, taking the narrow steps one at a time. They had every intention of replacing the pull-down ladder with a set of real stairs but couldn't until they'd made the big reveal. Otherwise Amy would've caught on to their surprise before they were ready.

Rhys joined them in the attic, standing tall now that he could.

It had taken some work, but they'd managed to restructure the joists to allow for headroom before they insulated and Sheetrocked the space. Air conditioning and heating ducts had also been run, ensuring Amy would be comfortable up here whenever she was in the space. And though it wasn't as big as they'd hoped it would be, Rhys knew it was plenty big for Amy to retreat to when she needed to.

"Oh, my God," she exclaimed, her hand covering her mouth as she stared around. "What...?"

"We thought you might like a space of your own," Wolfe informed her, gesturing to the room, which was now complete.

"Wolfe built the bookshelves and the benches himself," Rhys told her. "I was able to provide the reading material."

Amy's gaze skimmed over the shelves of books that lined both sides of the room.

It wasn't an enormous space, but it held a comfortable reading chair and probably more books than the local library. They'd added a few furnishings like a rug and a lamp, which they'd secretly questioned Amy about in the past couple of months. For all intents and purposes, she had approved everything in the room, although they'd attempted to conceal their quest.

"What do you think?" Wolfe asked, turning to face Amy.

Rhys peered over and that was when he saw the one thing he hadn't expected.

Tears.

AMY HAD TRIED TO HOLD THE TEARS back because she knew they would freak out Rhys and Wolfe, but she couldn't contain them. From the very moment she stepped foot into this space, she'd been overwhelmed with a joy she hadn't realized she could feel. Any gift they gave her would've been perfect, regardless of what it was. But this? Nothing could compare to what they'd done. This was hers. A space just for her because they loved her enough to know she needed to retreat from time to time.

Her heart … well, it was officially overflowing and the tears were her release valve.

"This is amazing," she whispered on a sob.

She honestly had no idea what this space had looked like before they'd done this, but she knew it had been where they stored things like the Christmas tree and ornaments, as well as a few other things they didn't use often.

"We'll be putting in stairs," Wolfe blurted, his gaze concerned. "That way you don't have to walk up the rickety ladder every time. We just … uh … we just didn't want to ruin the surprise."

Amy nodded, wiping the tears streaming down her cheeks.

"Is there a problem?" Rhys asked.

"No," she said quickly. "God, no. It's ... wonderful."

There was no denying she loved to read, but she rarely had the opportunity because whenever she tried, there was always too much going on at home. When she would sit in the living room, the television was usually on. When she would sneak into the bedroom, one of them would prove to be a distraction she couldn't ignore. Simply put, the house wasn't all that big, so finding a corner wasn't easy.

But this...

She took a step, then another, moving around the room, running her fingers over the bookshelves. Handmade bookshelves, which had been stained, sealed, and lacquered. The perfect complement to a wonderfully soothing space.

"You had no idea?" Wolfe asked.

Amy peered over. "About what? This?" She shook her head. "I mean, I knew y'all were up to something, but I would've never guessed this."

"There's a small fridge that'll hold those cold coffee drinks you like," Rhys said, pointing to the far corner of the room.

"Unfortunately, we couldn't add a bathroom," Wolfe noted.

Amy laughed. "This is perfect. Absolutely perfect."

"Yeah?"

She nodded enthusiastically, peering from one man to the other. "Absolutely."

She could see the triumph in their gazes. They were proud of themselves, as they should be. This truly was the greatest gift she'd ever received.

Which made her realize that the gifts she got them would pale in comparison.

"What's wrong?" Rhys asked, reaching for her hand and tugging her close.

She stared up at him. "I ... uh ... I didn't get you anything this nice."

He barked a laugh and pulled her into a hug. "Actually, you did."

Confused, she held on to him. "What does that mean?"

Wolfe moved in behind her, his arms coming around them as his mouth lowered near her ear. "You, Amy. You're our gift."

"The only thing we need," Rhys agreed, his words soft in her other ear.

Warmth filled her chest and her heart swelled.

Again.

No Longer Christmas but Still a Miracle

Phoenix, Tarik, and Mia from *A Million Tiny Pieces*

Sometimes making a decision and jumping in with both feet is the only thing to do. Phoenix learns that firsthand after a special request from his wife and husband.

Wednesday, December 29, 2021

"IT'S MY UNDERSTANDING YOU'RE IN A GOOD position for the playoffs this year."

Phoenix Pierce looked over, the man's words barely registering. The playoffs? It was December. The playoffs weren't until June of next year. Why the hell would he be thinking about the playoffs right now?

"You always were the humble kind," the man said.

"Yeah. Humble," he muttered, tossing back the rest of his drink before turning on his barstool.

Clearly, drowning his sorrows in whiskey was getting him nowhere, and the last thing he wanted to do was shoot the shit with a perfect stranger.

What he should've been doing was spending the evening with Mia and Tarik, getting a good night's rest before they headed back to Austin for the New Year's celebration Mia had talked him into putting on this year. When she had first approached him with the idea, he'd wanted to veto it. Of course, his wife was good at anticipating his moves, so she had already worked out the details, adding the one thing she knew he couldn't refuse: charity. Yep, his wife had decided to charge a relatively nice cover charge, every penny of it going to charity.

She was a sneaky one, there was no doubt about that. And because of that, he was responsible for an event that was getting enough press to ensure it was an epic moment in history. Probably had a lot to do with the fact that the Austin Arrows hockey players would be in attendance. The very same hockey team the man was claiming was headed for the playoffs, a prediction that was far too early to make.

Phoenix stared down into his glass and wondered when he'd become so judgmental.

He rapped his knuckles on the wooden bar top to get the bartender's attention. When the man looked over, Phoenix offered a nod, received one in return. He was a regular at this hotel, so the bartender was used to seeing him, billing his drinks to his account. Granted, he hadn't spent much time in a bar as of late. No, ever since he settled down with Mia and Tarik, Phoenix hadn't needed to use alcohol as a confidant.

Yet here he was and he had only himself to blame for his current mood.

As he headed for the elevator that would take him to the penthouse suite, Phoenix recalled the conversation he'd had with Mia a few months ago. The one where she had discreetly mentioned having a baby and he had nearly blown his top.

A baby?

How in the world did his wife expect them to have a baby? How did you raise a baby to have three parents? And who would be the father?

No sooner had she mentioned it than those and a million other questions started a repeat through his mind. Worse than the questions was the fact that he didn't have any answers. He didn't know how to raise a child in a normal, two-person household, much less with two fathers and one mother. And he couldn't fathom how Tarik was so easily on board with the idea.

Of course, Phoenix had done what he did best and ignored it like it would merely go away. He knew better, and he knew they both deserved an answer, but he wasn't sure how he was supposed to make a decision like this. Did he want kids? At one point, he'd never imagined he would be married. Certainly not to a man and a woman. The thought of having children... Although the logistics confused the shit out of him, he knew ultimately that he wanted children with Mia and Tarik. Hell, he wanted to give them everything they wanted. He just wasn't sure how to come to terms with it.

When he reached the top floor, Phoenix took a deep breath and exited the elevator. He stepped into the suite and found all the lights were off. The city skyline provided enough light to see since the curtains in the living room and dining area were still open. He paused there for a moment and stared out.

Being the owner of the Austin Arrows hockey team, Phoenix had gotten used to hotel rooms for a majority of the year. Each one knew him personally, knew what he preferred, what his husband and wife preferred, and always saw that they got what they needed. But for him, it was now just another stop in an endless loop that went on and on year after year.

Was he really complaining about his life? About his wealth? His happiness? Because at the root of it, he was happy. He loved Mia and Tarik and they'd established a comfortable, albeit busy, life.

Would they stop traveling with the team if they had a baby? Or would he be left to go out on his own, away from them so Tarik and Mia could stay home?

The thought didn't sit well and the questions were only more on the long, long list he couldn't answer.

His attention was snagged by sounds coming from the bedroom. They were sounds he'd gotten intimately familiar with over the years. Sounds of Mia being pleasured by Tarik. Just hearing them had the chaos in his head easing, his cock rising to attention.

With a practiced ease, Phoenix unknotted his tie as he headed toward the bedroom. He paused in the doorway and took in the scene. Mia was laid out across the bed, Tarik's face between her legs. Her breasts were thrust upward, her arms straining as she gripped the comforter and bowed her back, clearly enjoying Tarik's oral ministrations.

"God, yes," she whimpered. "More. Please more."

Tarik's rough grumble sounded, making Phoenix's cock swell even more.

He fucking loved watching the two of them together. No matter how many times he saw them, it was like the first time. An erotic assault on the senses that never ceased to amaze him by how hot it made him.

He must've made a sound because Tarik paused in his feast to look over.

Their eyes met across the dim room, but even from there, Phoenix could see the heat in Tarik's golden eyes.

Mia's attention shifted next, and Phoenix's gaze traveled over her sexy curves until he met her gaze. She smiled sweetly and gestured for him to join them.

It would've been easy for him to hang on to his frustration, to saunter into the bathroom and hide out in the shower for a while. He was still reeling from her request for a baby, and he wanted nothing more than to hold on to that fear and anger for a little while.

Unfortunately, Phoenix's willpower was only so great, and it had never defeated his desire to get close to them.

He pushed off the wall as he tugged the silk tie from beneath his collar, resigning himself to enjoying this moment while he was lucky enough to have it.

As soon as Mia noticed Phoenix standing in the doorway, her desire ratcheted up tenfold. That was the case every time she was presented with the opportunity to have the two men she loved with her like this. They turned her on in ways she had never expected, and even now, nearly seven years into their relationship, her body reacted in the same way it had all those years ago.

Crooking her finger to encourage Phoenix to join them, Mia watched him intently. Or rather, she tried right up until the blessed warmth of Tarik's mouth returned to her pussy, his tongue caressing her clit gently at first, coaxing the firestorm of intensity before he sensually assaulted her from all angles. He added a finger, pushing it deep inside as his lips latched on to her clit, his devious tongue thrashing.

Mia gripped the comforter, her back bowing again as she tried to hang out, wanting to endure the onslaught for as long as possible because it felt so damn good.

She was vaguely aware of Phoenix discarding his suit, laying each article he removed over the armchair to be dealt with later. When he was finally naked, he strolled toward her, looking every bit the sexy businessman even when he donned nothing at all.

Curious as to which direction their encounter would take, Mia panted, fighting the onslaught that was the prelude to her orgasm as Phoenix joined her on the bed, lying beside her, his hand cupping her knee and widening her legs while Tarik continued to feast.

"You ready to come?" Phoenix taunted, his warm hand curling over her breast, teasing her with the gentlest of caresses, making her skin prickle as she short-circuited from the pleasure of it all.

"Not yet," she bit out, fighting as much as she could despite the fact she knew it was futile.

Phoenix's hand slid down over her stomach, down her thigh, then between her legs. She was aware of his finger sliding alongside Tarik's, pushing inside her, filling her impossibly full. They both fingered her while Tarik forced her closer and closer to the edge with his tongue.

"Oh, God!" she cried out, unable to hold on any longer. Her back bowed, her pussy clamping down on the two fingers thrusting inside her. Her clit pulsed and throbbed as ecstasy coursed through her veins.

When the wave crashed through her, her bones and muscles turned to mush as she fell onto the bed. Her lungs worked overtime to compensate for the devastation, and she found herself smiling.

"That was the first one," Tarik said, crawling up over her, his smile mirroring hers as he turned his attention to Phoenix. "Taste her on my mouth."

Phoenix didn't hesitate, reaching for Tarik, his hand curling around behind his head as he pulled him closer, their lips crashing together. Mia was enraptured by the sight. She loved watching them together. What it was about them when they came together in the heat of passion, she couldn't quite explain, but it reignited the flame within her.

Wanting to ensure they were aware of her presence, Mia reached between them, gripping each of their cocks in a fist and stroking lightly. She loved pushing them, and by using gentle caresses, she would succeed.

After all, it was only fair.

TARIK KISSED PHOENIX, THRUSTING HIS TONGUE INTO the man's mouth, letting him know with his kiss just how much he wanted him there.

Things had been a bit off with them lately, ever since Mia had mentioned wanting to have a baby a few months ago. While Tarik was on board with the idea, he knew Phoenix was not. And while Tarik wanted to give Mia everything she could ever want, he knew this was not something he could decide for them, but at the same time, Tarik wasn't willing to allow it to come between them, either. He wasn't about to let Phoenix put up those emotional walls simply because he didn't know how to process what was going on between them.

"She tastes good, doesn't she?" Tarik taunted, pulling his lips away.

"Better than good," Phoenix agreed, turning his head and finding Mia's mouth.

Tarik watched them, his body burning hotter the longer their kiss lasted. He loved seeing them together like this. At times, he wondered if he could get off simply by watching and not joining in. Not that he was in a state of mind to find out now. Not with his cock currently gliding through Mia's smooth, soft palm. She was driving him absolutely insane and she knew it.

Phoenix pulled back with a groan, falling onto his back and gripping his cock firmly. Tarik shifted to his knees, staring down at Mia as she continued to stroke them both.

"You better be careful," Phoenix warned, his gaze also lingering on Mia's hand as it worked him. "Keep that up and I'll come."

"Isn't that the goal?" she asked with a giggle.

"Only if you want me to come in your hand and not in your tight little pussy."

Tarik's eyes shot to her face, loving the way she inhaled sharply, clearly turned on by Phoenix's dirty words.

"Is that what you want?" Tarik asked her.

"No," she said quickly. "I want you both to fuck me."

It was Tarik's turn to draw a sharp breath, his cock jerking at her crass words. Their sweet Mia was usually more ladylike with her requests, but this … oh, yeah, Tarik liked her like this.

"We can certainly oblige," he told her, glancing at Phoenix, wanting to take his cues from the man.

He didn't have to wait because Phoenix moved quickly, reaching for Mia and pulling her over him.

"We definitely can," Phoenix agreed. "Sit on my cock, Mia."

As soon as Tarik realized which route they were taking, he reached for the nightstand where he'd stashed lube and condoms.

"Not necessary," Phoenix said gruffly.

Tarik paused, looking over, curious as to what he had in mind then.

Phoenix's eyes were locked on Mia's face. "Sit on my cock," he repeated.

"Condom," she said, as though reminding Phoenix that she was not currently on birth control.

"Sit. On. My. Cock."

Tarik's chest squeezed as he processed what Phoenix was ultimately saying by his gruff demand. Without a condom, there was a risk she would get pregnant.

Mia paused, her hands flat on Phoenix's chest. "This could—"

"We're gonna fuck you at the same time," Phoenix interrupted. "Both of us. In your pussy."

Tarik's cock jerked at the thought. They'd only done this a couple of times before because it was not exactly as easy as it sounded.

"No protection," he tacked on.

Refusing to be left out of this conversation—which wasn't much of a conversation—Tarik moved closer, pushing Phoenix's legs wider as he positioned himself behind Mia.

He stared over her shoulder at the man he loved. "You sure this is what you want?"

Tarik could see the frustration on Phoenix's face. If the man could avoid the conversation, he would.

Phoenix jerked his chin.

"Say it," Tarik demanded.

Phoenix's gaze bounced between them. "Yes."

Tarik was surprised by the conviction in his tone.

"I want to make you both happy. Whatever that means."

"That's not how this works," Mia said, lifting up and blocking Tarik's view of Phoenix's face.

Phoenix huffed and flopped down on the bed. "Fine, then why don't I leave you to it. Just let me—"

"Say it," Tarik snapped, not willing to let Phoenix retreat. Clearly he'd come to a decision and now Tarik wanted him to own up to it.

Phoenix opened his eyes, looked at Mia first, then Tarik. "I want a family with you both. I want children. Two, three, twelve. It doesn't matter."

Mia's shocked inhale drained some of the tension. "I beg to differ. Twelve is way too many."

Tarik's chest loosened as he leaned around Mia, met Phoenix's gaze. "Then let's make a baby."

"Yes," Phoenix said firmly. "Let's."

MIA WAS STILL TRYING TO PROCESS THE words when she felt the blunt head of Phoenix's cock press against her. She probably should've questioned what his motivation was, why he was coming to this conclusion now when she'd brought up the subject months ago and they had yet to discuss it further.

Only she didn't want to ask questions. In fact, she wanted nothing other than to feel Phoenix and Tarik inside her, loving her. This was all she'd ever wanted, the two of them, the family they'd built. Sure, she wanted children, too, but Mia always suspected she would be all right if they didn't have any. She had a wonderful life with these men and she wasn't about to claim otherwise.

But a baby...?

Her body stretched as Phoenix pushed his hips up, filling her. There were no barriers between them and the heat of him was glorious.

"Phoenix..."

"Take all of me, baby," he crooned, pulling her down toward him. "Let us love you."

She sighed and relaxed against him, her inner muscles clenching around the delicious intrusion while Tarik moved behind her. She felt the press of his cock between her legs, felt the stretch as he aligned his cock with Phoenix's and pushed forward. Mia took a deep breath, relaxed, and allowed him to slide inside her. Then she was overwhelmed by the sensation of two cocks stretching her impossibly wide. It was more than she could handle, but at the same time, it felt ridiculously good.

But it didn't last long because there was only one way this worked and that was for them to alternate. Mia held on tight as they began to fuck her, whispering crude words in her ear as they alternately thrust, leaving her filled at all times. The friction was intense. So intense she thought she might lose it at any second, but she held on, not wanting it to end.

"Fuck. So tight," Phoenix rumbled against her ear. "Your pussy filled with both our cocks ... it's fucking perfect."

Yeah, what he said.

Their words drifted off, morphing into little more than strangled grunts and satisfied moans as the three of them moved together almost as one.

Mia was the first to succumb to the intensity, her body tensing as the fibers that made up her being became electrically charged. When she came, it was with both their names falling from her lips. Phoenix was the next to let go, driving into her, his cock pulsing hotly. No sooner had he pulled out than Tarik drove in deep and groaned long and low in her ear as he came, too.

"Oh, my God," she whispered softly, smiling as she relaxed against Phoenix. "That was..."

"Amazing?" Phoenix inserted.

"Incredible?" Tarik added.

"Yeah," she said softly. "Exactly that."

And to think, they might soon have their very own Christmas miracle.

Kicking Off the New Year Right

Trey Walker and Magnus Storm from *Brantley Walker: Off the Books series*

Although he's insistent they keep their relationship on the DL, Trey decides to make the first move. That decision might just change things between him and Magnus forever.

Friday, December 31, 2021

TREY WALKER WOULD ADMIT HE HADN'T KNOWN what to expect when he received an invitation to a New Year's Eve party at his brother's house. Brantley wasn't exactly the social type, so to find out the man was inviting a dozen or so people over to ring in the new year had shocked him.

Of course, when he had learned the party was actually Reese's idea, it had made more sense. Brantley's boyfriend was certainly more sociable, and he was much better with people.

When he arrived at eight forty, a little more than *fashionably* late, Trey hadn't intended to stay for long. He would've been content to go home and spend the rest of this year and the first part of the next in his quiet house, alone with his television remote. And perhaps a warm body, if he could convince Magnus to skip whatever party he was going to get himself invited to.

However, since seeing Magnus hadn't been an option— Trey damn sure did not intend to look needy—he had pulled on a nice shirt, his best pair of Wranglers, and his boots and headed over. When he arrived, it was to find that there were more than a dozen people crammed inside Brantley's four-bedroom farmhouse. Hell, there were even some spilling out onto the front and back porches, a few huddled under the outdoor heater, others content with the reasonable Texas temperatures.

"I didn't think you were comin'," Brantley said by way of greeting as he approached Trey near the front door.

"Wasn't about to let you give me shit for standin' you up," he told his brother.

Brantley smirked. "I'll still give you shit."

Of course he would.

"Grab a beer or chance one of those mixed drinks Bryn's mixin' up in the kitchen."

"Bryn's here?" Trey hadn't realized this was going to be a family affair.

"Mom, Dad, sisters, brothers…" Brantley nodded. "Reese went all out, invited the whole family."

Well, not the whole family, Trey knew. The Walker clan was a significant one, and their little branch of the family tree was minuscule in the grand scheme of things.

"Oh, and Magnus is here," Brantley said as he strolled away, a knowing grin plastered on his face.

Trey pretended not to hear him. He damn sure wasn't going to give his brother fuel for whatever hell he decided to give Trey in the coming days and weeks. God knew whatever happened at this party would set the tone for the jokes and the ridicule.

Then again, it worked both ways. Trey wasn't above giving his brothers and sisters shit, either.

"Trey!" Bryn shouted when he made it to the kitchen, where half a dozen people were crowded around the island, watching as Bryn worked an enormous blender. She was laughing it up right up until the lid on the thing shot up, sending frozen margaritas out like lava from a volcano.

Surprisingly, everyone found it amusing. Even Reese.

And that right there set the tone for the rest of the evening.

Saturday, January 1, 2022

TREY SPENT THE MAJORITY OF THE NIGHT mingling with co-workers, harassing his sisters, laughing with his brothers, shooting the shit with his mother and father, and ultimately enjoying himself. They had counted down and toasted the new year as a group, everyone cheering and hoping for a better year to come. The last couple had been a shit show, so Trey figured something had to give.

As it rolled into early morning, Trey had to admit, being here with the people he cared about was a hell of a lot better than spending the night alone.

Then again, if he hadn't been alone, if Magnus had chosen to come over rather than come here and give Trey shit by taunting him at every turn with those subtle glances and knowing grins, Trey would've hightailed it out of here a long time ago. As it was, Trey had remained at the party long after Magnus had left despite Magnus taunting him, promising to come by if he left with him.

Although he had accepted he was having an affair with a much younger man, that didn't mean Trey wanted anyone else to know. Not only because Magnus was twenty-five and Trey was thirty-seven. No, Trey's main reason was because, as long as no one else knew, then it couldn't be serious. The last thing Trey needed was to fall for another man. He'd already proven he had a shitty track record when it came to romance, and he had no intention of adding to that long list of failures.

So here he was, sitting on his couch, debating on whether he should go to sleep or stick it out in hopes that Magnus would show up. He usually did. Of course, Trey got the feeling tonight would be the night Magnus stood his ground, stayed away just to punish Trey for putting his foot down.

He couldn't necessarily blame the guy. After all, Magnus had put forth every ounce of effort up to this point. Trey had stood by his decision to keep a safe distance, and Magnus had simply railroaded over his good intentions.

And Trey had let him.

Perhaps he should make the first move for once. He could go over to Camp K-9, surprise Magnus with an impromptu visit at three in the morning. As long as they didn't get a case, he wouldn't have to work today, so he didn't have to worry about how much sleep he got.

Before he could come up with a rational, well-thought-out decision, Trey was on his feet, snagging his keys from the table, tucking his wallet into his back pocket, and grabbing his cell phone. He was in his truck and heading down the road five minutes later. Fifteen more and he was pulling into the long, winding drive that led to Camp K-9, the boarding and training facility owned and operated by Magnus Storme.

When he neared the house that sat in front of the Camp K-9 building, Trey noticed it was completely dark. Not even the porch light was on.

He continued past, pulling up to the metal building that housed the office and some of the training space. There was a light on inside, so he cut the engine but didn't immediately get out of his truck.

Trey thought back to the first and only time he'd come here. It had been at Reese's urging because Trey had wondered whether or not Magnus's search and rescue dogs might be able to track down Juliet Prince during their hunt for her.

"Did you have a reason for bein' here?" Magnus asked. "Or did you come to ogle me and my dogs?"

Hating that the younger man called him out, Trey glowered at him when he spoke. "You've heard about what's goin' on?"

"I did, yes. I'm sorry for your loss."

Trey instantly looked at the floor, grief over Kylie's death filling him. "Thanks."

"I take it your team's lookin' for the woman responsible? The one who kidnapped the little girl and murdered that girl's mother."

Trey nodded. "We've got an active team tryin' to determine where she is. We know she's in the area, just don't have an exact location."

"By in the area, you mean what? Central Texas? Coyote Ridge? Taylor? Embers Ridge? What?"

"Yes."

Magnus chuckled. "Not exactly helpful. And unfortunately, unless I have a vicinity in which to work, I can't be of much help. I assume that's why you're here? My services?"

Trey felt his face heat at the double entendre. "Yeah. Your ... uh"— *Trey cleared his throat, motioned toward the long counter with the Camp K-9 sign behind it*—*"services. I..." More throat clearing. "We thought you might be able to... I just... I wanted to ask."*

That had been a clusterfuck of a meeting between them, but evidently Magnus hadn't held it against Trey, because shortly thereafter, they'd started up this clandestine affair, the one where Magnus came over in the dark of night and slipped out before dawn.

And here Trey was, turning this into something more, something it shouldn't be. He needed to turn around, go back home, and pretend he wasn't stupid enough to make the first move when there weren't any moves that needed to be made.

However, his brain was on one wavelength, his body on another, because the next thing Trey knew, he was getting out of the truck. Taking a deep breath, he walked to the door, willing his heart to slow its painful thump in his chest. This was a first for him, something he'd promised himself he would never do. Leaving it to Magnus to make the first move kept him at a safe distance. By doing this, Trey was taking the first step.

He paused at the door.

He should turn around and go home. He didn't belong here.

Something more powerful than his thoughts had him reaching for the door. He pulled it open slowly, trying to avoid making the bell overhead ring and announce his presence.

Trey came to an abrupt halt at the scene before him.

There was Magnus, his arms around a woman, her head resting on his shoulder. She appeared to be distraught. Crying. But the way Magnus was holding her … it was…

Trey didn't know how to describe it, but it reminded him of the fact that Magnus was openly bisexual, that he enjoyed both men and women and made no apologies for it.

Magnus must've heard him, because he turned his head, peering over and meeting Trey's gaze briefly. He didn't release the woman, waiting for her to calm down.

Trey had plenty of time to leave, to walk right back out the door and into the night. It would've been easy to get in his truck, go home, pretend this never happened. He could avoid Magnus, use this as an excuse to put an end to their intimate encounters.

But something kept him there, had him watching the way Magnus's hand cradled the back of the woman's head, his fingers tucked into her sleek golden-blond hair in a gesture that spoke of intimacy that went far beyond friendship. Who was she? Why was she here?

He met Magnus's gaze, tried to read him, to gauge what was going on here, but he couldn't. Their eyes locked and held for long moments, but neither of them spoke. It was in those few brief seconds that an image flashed in Trey's mind, vivid and clear. Magnus with this woman, the two of them naked, Magnus pushing inside her, slow, deep strokes as they panted and moaned. Trey felt his body heat, the mental image making his cock thicken in his jeans.

Christ. Was he turned on by the thought of Magnus with a woman?

"I'm sorry," the woman mumbled softly, stepping back. "I shouldn't be here, I know."

Magnus released her, his hands sliding to her arms, going downward until he was holding her hands. "Don't ever be sorry. I'm always here if you need me."

She sobbed softly, then pulled away, wiping her eyes with the heels of her palms.

Trey cleared his throat, trying to announce his presence without scaring her. It didn't stop her from jerking around, her eyes slamming into him.

It was then Trey noticed she had a swollen lip and what looked to be a black eye forming. If it hadn't been for those marks, she would've been possibly the most beautiful woman he'd ever seen. Her soft features were smooth, rounded, her eyes a brilliant blue. She looked young. Early- or maybe mid-twenties. Young and innocently beautiful.

He instantly shot a look to Magnus.

"Ava, this is Trey Walker. Trey, Ava March. She's … a friend."

"Are you all right?" Trey asked on instinct, pained by the sight of her face. It was clear someone had hit her, and they hadn't pulled the punch, either.

Ava sniffed, her voice soft, sweet when she said, "Yes. I'm sorry for comin' here."

"No you're not," Magnus countered, taking her arm and pulling her back to him. "I think you should stay here tonight. You can sleep in my bed. I'll bunk out here."

Ava was shaking her head. "I can't do that."

"You can and you will." Magnus met Trey's gaze, something that looked a lot like a dare flashing in his eyes.

What? Did Magnus think Trey was going to get upset? He had no claim to the man. If he wanted to have this woman … this stunningly beautiful, this *much-closer-to-Magnus's-age-than-Trey* woman sleep in his bed, who was he to stand in his way?

Ava pulled back again, wiping her eyes and steeling her spine as she glanced over at Trey momentarily then turned her attention back to Magnus. "I appreciate it."

Magnus nodded. "Go on in the house, get settled. I'll check on you in a little while."

"It's nice to meet you," Ava said as she stepped toward the door.

Trey moved out of the way, forced a smile. "Likewise."

When the door closed behind her, sealing Trey in the building with Magnus, he turned to the man only to see that Magnus had closed the distance between them.

Before Trey could tell him he should go, Magnus had him up against the wall, their lips fused.

As strong as he wanted to be, Trey couldn't seem to resist this man when he did things like that. So instead of shoving him away like he intended, Trey gripped his hips and jerked him forward, thrusting his tongue into Magnus's mouth, taking control of the kiss, eager to sate this lust that seemed to be a constant burn in his veins.

Trey wanted to strip Magnus bare, to bend him over the counter and fuck him until they were both replete, both too exhausted to think about feelings and emotions and shit that Trey had no business thinking about. He knew Magnus would go willingly, too. He would take Trey into his body without argument and enjoy every magnificent second of it.

Instead of making the logical choice to fuck Magnus blind, Trey heard himself growl, "Who is she, Magnus?"

Magnus panted as he nipped Trey's lower hip. "A friend. Why? You jealous?"

"Fuck no." He wasn't. He couldn't be.

Magnus's hand went between them, grinding against the hard ridge of Trey's erection. "Did I do this?"

Trey didn't respond. He damn sure wasn't going to admit he'd found something strangely erotic about seeing Magnus with that woman. Definitely not after he'd realized someone had hurt her.

"What happened to her?" Trey asked, realizing that woman's safety was far more pressing than this lust coursing in his veins.

"She's safe now," Magnus said, his tone reassuring.

"Safe from who?"

Magnus pulled back, stared up into his face. "Why're you here, Trey?"

That was a damn good question. Why the fuck *was* he here?

MAGNUS FORCED HIMSELF TO PULL BACK FROM Trey, waiting for an answer to his question.

He could admit, when he saw Trey standing in the office, he'd been pleasantly surprised by his arrival even if the man's timing was horrible. If it hadn't been for Ava coming by, hurt both physically and emotionally, seeking the friendship and security Magnus could provide her, he would've been all over the man, taunting him about giving in and finally putting forth an effort in this relationship.

Damn good way to kick off the new year, that was for sure.

"I shouldn't be here," Trey finally muttered.

"That seems to be the theme tonight," Magnus remarked, remembering how Ava had said the same thing.

"You've got company. I should go."

Magnus nodded, wondering if Trey was expecting him to beg him to stay. He wanted to, sure. And that was something he'd come to terms with over the past nine months or so. Magnus could not deny this ridiculous attraction he had to Trey. It didn't seem to matter how many times they fucked, how many encounters they had where Trey proved there was only one thing he wanted from Magnus, he still found himself coming back.

Which meant this was monumental. Trey had come to him.

"Go ahead, ask me again," Magnus taunted.

Trey took a step toward the door. "Ask you what?"

"Who she is, why she's here, what I intend to do with her now that she's in my bed?"

Magnus watched Trey's expression shutter. He was closing himself off as he always did, refusing to acknowledge that he gave a shit. That was something else Magnus had gotten used to over these past months, and to be honest, it didn't bother him. No, it simply made him want the man more, eager to show Trey that they had something here, and no matter if they pretended otherwise, it was progressing into something more.

Of course, Magnus would not say that aloud. He wasn't a fucking idiot. That would be the fastest way to get Trey to bolt.

"You said she's a friend," Trey stated, his lips a hard line.

"She is." Magnus tilted his head. "You want to know how friendly we are?"

"No."

Magnus smirked at the lie. "Suit yourself."

Trey's eyes narrowed. "I'm gonna go."

"You've said that already."

"I mean it this time."

"Do you?"

Trey's expression went cold and then he was turning toward the door.

Magnus had known he'd pushed a little harder than usual. He'd gotten relatively good at reading Trey's tipping point, but this time he'd overshot the mark. Probably had something to do with Ava being here. Quite possibly the fact that Magnus hadn't given in and told Trey she was just a friend, nothing more.

Before Trey could reach the handle, Magnus launched himself forward, gripping Trey's arm, pulling him to a stop. As was usually the case when he became the aggressor, Trey reacted in kind. He spun around, grabbed Magnus by the shirt, and pressed him up against the wall.

"I think it's time we call this," Trey ground out, his eyes hard as they locked with Magnus's.

Sarcasm was always Magnus's instant reaction. It was something he'd learned early on, a way of dealing with rejection. Before Trey, he'd never bothered to rein himself in, hence the reason he always found himself alone, running off anyone who might've become important to him. Trey was the first man Magnus had ever felt something for, even if he couldn't admit it to him.

"No," he countered, reaching up and gripping the back of Trey's neck. "We're not done yet."

"We are. We've been—"

Magnus kissed him. Hard. He held on to Trey's neck until Trey leaned into him, their tongues thrashing violently, the heat that always churned between them becoming an inferno, coalescing into a firestorm that threatened to take them both out.

As usual, Magnus melted against him, giving up all resistance, submitting completely to Trey. He knew it was what the man needed, and he was more than willing to give in if it meant Trey wouldn't push him away.

While their tongues dueled, Magnus roughly jerked the button on Trey's jeans, yanked down the zipper until his cock was freed from the denim. He took him in his fist, curling his fingers around his thick shaft, and stroked until Trey hissed, releasing Magnus's lips.

"Fuck," Trey groaned, his hips pumping as he fucked Magnus's hand.

Magnus had learned exactly what to do to make Trey's eyes roll back, exactly how to handle him to make him succumb to the pleasure. It had been a challenge at first, one he'd wanted to conquer. Now it was something he craved.

"You want to come in my hand or my mouth?" Magnus taunted, breathing hard as they both watched his hand working Trey's cock.

"Mouth," Trey grunted. "Put your fuckin' mouth on me, Magnus."

Without hesitation, Magnus slid down the wall, dropping to his knees and taking Trey to the root. He sucked and bobbed, working him the way Trey loved. And when Trey's cock jerked and he came down Magnus's throat, he swallowed him down, fighting the urge to come in his jeans because this man … this fucking man could set him off like no one he'd ever met.

Magnus remained on his knees when Trey took a step back, tucked his spent cock into his jeans.

Their eyes met briefly, neither of them saying anything.

There was nothing to say. Trey had gotten what he needed from Magnus, and Magnus had ensured the tether that kept them coming back to one another was still intact.

Without a word, Trey walked out the door and into the night.

Magnus had expected no less.

I hope you enjoyed these short stories! I had so much fun catching up with the characters.

Don't forget, if you enjoyed any of the short stories and would like more, be sure to visit Nicole's website and vote for them on the Naughty Holidays 2021 Poll. One set of characters from the Naughty Holidays 2021 book will receive a full-length book in 2022.

The holiday poll will be open until December 31, 2021

ACKNOWLEDGMENTS

This book came to be in large part thanks to my fabulous readers, specifically those who interact with me frequently in Nicole Nation on Facebook. Thanks to their input and suggestions, many of these stories formed.

- o *__Holiday Road Trip__* (Grace, Grant, Lane) was inspired by Jackie Walton's suggestion about an RV road trip.

- o *__The Perfect Gift__* (Wolfe, Rhys, Amy) was inspired by Karen Bartholomew's suggestion about giving their wife a gift of a room dedicated for her relaxing time.

- o *__Naughty Cruise__* (Landon, Langston, Luci) was inspired by Christine LaCombe's suggestion of a sex-related cruise specifically for throuples.

- o *__Making the Most of It__* (Hunter, Dani, Kye) was inspired by Bethany Livengood-Lazzara's suggestion about one person being called away for work right before the holiday.

- o *__Cabin by Candlelight__* (Logan, Sam, Elijah) was inspired by Amy Casey's specific suggestion for this throuple and a holiday getaway.

- o *__No Longer Christmas but still a Miracle__* (Phoenix, Mia, Tarik) was inspired by Sue LeBlanc's suggestion about a throuple dealing with a potential future baby.

Other suggestions were made (although not used) by Christine McCarthy, Zena Anne Foster, Linda Reitz, Janet Seeley, Shannon Stahl, Terry Sasada, Cheryl Hayes, Jaki Gardner, Vicki Harris, Christine Geier, Michelle Mills, Michelle Rautens, and Helle Feldstedt. And as always, my good friend Chancy Powley helped things along by listening to me ramble on and on. She's good like that.

I also want to give a huge shout out to:

The Nicole Nation Street Team. Ladies, your daily promotion and support fills my heart with so much love. You are a blessing to me, each and every one of you.

My copyeditor, Amy. Punctuation and grammar… well, that's not my strong suit. But it is yours and you are truly remarkable at what you do. You simply amaze me and I am so glad that I found you.

Nicole Nation 2.0 for the constant support and love. This group of ladies has kept me going for so long, I'm not sure I'd know what to do without them.

And, of course, YOU, the reader. Your emails, messages, posts, comments, tweets… they mean more to me than you can imagine. I thrive on hearing from you, knowing that my characters and my stories have touched you in some way keeps me going. I've been known to shed a tear or two when reading an email because you simply bring so much joy to my life with your support. I thank you for that.

ABOUT NICOLE EDWARDS

New York Times and *USA Today* bestselling author Nicole Edwards lives in the suburbs of Austin, Texas with her husband and their youngest of three children. The two older ones have flown the coup, while the youngest recently graduated from high school. When Nicole is not writing about sexy alpha males and sassy, independent women, she can often be found with a book in hand or attempting to keep the dogs happy. You can find her hanging out on social media and interacting with her readers - even when she's supposed to be writing.

CONNECT WITH NICOLE

I hope you're as eager to get the information as I am to give it. Any one of these things is worth signing up for, or feel free to sign up for all. I promise to keep each one unique and interesting.

NIC NEWS: If you haven't signed up for my newsletter and you want to get notifications regarding preorders, new releases, giveaways, sales, etc, then you'll want to sign up. I promise not to spam your email, just get you the most important updates.

NICOLE'S BLOG: My blog is used for writer ramblings, which I am known to do from time to time. I will keep these separate from the newsletter updates or what I post in the Hot Sheet so that I don't duplicate in your inbox.

NN ON FACEBOOK: Join my reader group to interact with other readers, ask me questions, play fun weekly games, celebrate during release week, and enter exclusive giveaways!

INSTAGRAM: Basically, Instagram is where I post pictures of my dogs, so if you want to see epic cuteness, you should follow me.

TEXT: Want a simple, fast way to get updates on new releases? Sign up for text messaging. If you are in the U.S. simply text NICOLE to 64600. I promise not to spam your phone. This is just my way of letting you know what's happening because I know you're busy, but if you're anything like me, you always have your phone on you.

NAUGHTY & NICE SHOP: Not only does the shop have signed books, but there's fun merchandise, too. Plenty of naughty and nice options to go around. Find the shop on my website.

Website:	NicoleEdwards.me
Facebook:	/Author.Nicole.Edwards
Instagram:	NicoleEdwardsAuthor
BookBub:	/NicoleEdwardsAuthor

BY NICOLE EDWARDS

THE WALKERS

ALLURING INDULGENCE
Kaleb
Zane
Travis
Holidays with The Walker Brothers
Ethan
Braydon
Sawyer
Brendon

THE WALKERS OF COYOTE RIDGE
Curtis
Jared (a crossover novel)
Hard to Hold
Hard to Handle
Beau
Rex
A Coyote Ridge Christmas
Mack
Kaden & Keegan
Alibi (a crossover novel)

BRANTLEY WALKER: OFF THE BOOKS
All In
Without A Trace
Hide & Seek
Deadly Coincidence
Alibi (a crossover novel)

PIER 70
Reckless
Fearless
Speechless
Harmless
Clueless

SNIPER 1 SECURITY
Wait for Morning
Never Say Never
Tomorrow's Too Late

SOUTHERN BOY MAFIA/DEVIL'S PLAYGROUND
Beautifully Brutal
Without Regret
Beautifully Loyal
Without Restraint

STANDALONE NOVELS
Unhinged Trilogy
A Million Tiny Pieces
Inked on Paper
Bad Reputation
Bad Business

NAUGHTY HOLIDAY EDITIONS
2015
2016
2021